Confessions
of a
NOT IT *Girl*

Confessions
of a
NOT IT *Girl*

MELISSA KANTOR

HYPERION PAPERBACKS

NEW YORK

Copyright © 2004 by Melissa Kantor

Printed in the United States of America
First Hyperion Paperbacks edition, 2006

1 3 5 7 9 10 8 6 4 2

Library of Congress Cataloging-in-Publication Data on file.
ISBN 0-7868-1837-9 (tr.)
ISBN 0-7868-1808-5 (pbk.)
Visit www.hyperionbooksforchildren.com

TO BEN

CHAPTER ONE

Some people probably waste a lot of time wondering if they are destined to lead fabulous and exciting lives. I am not one of those people. I need look no further than my first name to know the answer.

A Quick Renaissance Quiz

1. Which of the following have you never heard of?
   (a) *Michelangelo*
   (b) *Leonardo da Vinci*
   (c) *Jan van Eyck*

2. Jan Miller is named after
   (a) *Michelangelo*
   (b) *Leonardo da Vinci*
   (c) *Jan van Eyck*

3. Jan van Eyck is a
   (a) *town*
   (b) *woman*
   (c) *man*

4. Jan van Eyck painted
   (a) *spectacular landscapes*
   (b) *magnificent frescoes*
   (c) *freaky, skinny giants with tiny heads*

If you answered (c) for all four, you're batting a thousand.

Welcome to my life.

Just in case you think things aren't bad enough, you should know that *Jan* is actually pronounced "Yahn." The only thing about my name I'm even remotely grateful for is everyone initially assumes it's pronounced "Jan," and I don't correct them. Well, I guess there's one other thing to be thankful for. My dad is an art history professor at Columbia University, and his all-time favorite painting is *The Garden of Earthly Delights*, by a guy named Hieronymus Bosch.

Jan is bad.

But it's not as bad as *Hieronymus*.

Walking home from the subway after school on Wednesday, I was so busy fantasizing about introducing myself with a normal name next year at college that I forgot to prepare for Brueghel's ritual assault. As a result, he almost knocked me on my butt when I opened the door. Brueghel, another hapless victim of my parents' nomenclature, like me and my brother Rogier, is a chocolate Lab and is without a doubt the dumbest animal in the entire world. People who come over usually try petting him for a minute because they're under the illusion it will get him to stop jumping, but it only works for as long as you're *actively* petting him. The second you stop, he just goes crazy again.

"Yahn, is that you?"

"Yeah, Mom."

"I'm just finishing up an e-mail, and then I'll be down. There's a message on the machine for you."

My mom produces documentary films, and for the past six months she's been working on one about teenage girls who got pregnant and decided to keep their babies. Last year when she started making the movie, we had this Big Talk, and she asked me all these questions about sex, and kept saying how she wanted me to feel I could come to her if there was anything I wanted to know, and how it was perfectly natural to be curious, and blah blah blah. The Big Talk took place right around the time *Chic* magazine named my best friend, Rebecca Larkin, one of Ten New York "It Girls," and so I made this joke about how if I got pregnant then my mom could put me in her movie, and I'd get to be famous, too.

Needless to say, she did not find this funny at all.

The message light was blinking on the answering machine in the kitchen. I hit PLAY, grabbed the seltzer out of the fridge, and took a swig directly from the bottle, something I do only when my mother is safely ensconced in her office on the third floor.

The first message was from my grandmother. "Hello. Hello?" There was a pause; my grandmother always sounds like she's never encountered an answering machine in her life. "Elizabeth, it's your mother. Are you there?" Pause. "So you're not there." Pause. "Hello?" Pause. "Okay, you're not there. Call me." Pause. "Okay." Then, as an afterthought, she repeated, "It's your mother."

It didn't seem as if there was another message on the

machine, and for a minute I worried my mom had meant for *me* to call my grandmother back, an activity about as enjoyable as retaking the SATs. But then there was another beep. "Hi, Jan, it's Sarah Gardner." My heart started to beat faster; Sarah Gardner is Josh's mom.

Josh is my new crush.

Well, I can't exactly say he's my *crush* because that would imply I only have one, and I do have a fairly significant crush on Tom Richmond. But lately, Josh has taken the lead in the Best Supporting Crush category.

I turned up the volume on the machine. "I absolutely *hate* to do this to you, but do you think you could *possibly* baby-sit Hannah Friday night? I know how *busy* you seniors are, and I know it's *completely* last minute." My mom says she can actually see the italics when Sarah talks. "But my regular baby-sitter's sick, and I have theater tickets I *hate* to lose. I think you have the number, but in case you don't, it's 555-9908."

Josh moved to New York from Seattle over the summer because his dad, whom he'd been living with, got a job in Tokyo. Well, he really moved *back* to New York, since he used to live here when he was a little kid. We were actually in the same first-grade class, but then he moved to Seattle. A few years later his mom and dad got divorced. When Sarah, her new husband, and their daughter, Hannah, came back to New York, I guess Josh didn't want to leave Seattle, so he stayed with his dad. Sophomore year I used to baby-sit Hannah every weekend, and whenever she talked about her brother in Seattle, I pictured some greasy guy in baggy jeans listening to grunge music, who slept with a skateboard under his pillow.

I saw Josh the first day of school, but I didn't realize who he was at first. Not that it mattered. I was way too busy flirting up a storm with Tom in history to care about there being some random new guy in my English class. The second day of school Josh introduced himself, and we talked for a minute, and then he said, "So maybe I'll see you sometime when you baby-sit Hannah." I told him I don't really baby-sit anymore, and he said, "Well, then, I guess I'll be hanging out by myself on Friday nights."

"I guess so," I said, thinking, *What a loser*.

But in retrospect there can be no doubt my usually accurate crush radar was malfunctioning when this conversation took place, because last Monday it suddenly began working properly.

I had agreed to stay after school to help Mrs. O'Connor carry boxes from the science office to the physics lab, and the job was turning out to be a nightmare. The lab and the office are practically in different time zones, and the pile of boxes (filled with stuff Mrs. O'Connor had probably been collecting since Prohibition) was wedged behind a metal cabinet. It didn't help that after every trip, I had to lock the lab door and then, when I returned with the next box, I had to stand there with it wedged between my hip and the wall while trying to figure out yet again which of the hundreds of keys on Mrs. O'Connor's key ring would unlock the door. I was on what must have been my millionth trip, searching for the key and hating Mrs. O'Connor, when a bunch of guys from the soccer team walked by. Some of them said hi to me, but in spite of the fact that I was about to drop a thousand pounds of equipment on my foot, they all kept walking. Except Josh.

"You need some help?" he asked.

"No thanks," I said. I was too angry at myself, Mrs. O'Connor, and the universe to say yes. In fact, I didn't even look up at him. I just kept searching for the right key.

"You sure?" he asked.

I found the key and opened the door. "I'm sure," I said, grabbing the box with both hands and glancing in his direction.

"Ah," he said, "what a girl won't do for a college rec."

And then, just before he turned and walked away, he smiled at me.

And instead of thinking, *What a loser*, I found myself thinking, *What a smile*.

I started dialing the number before Sarah finished saying it.

"Hi, Sarah, it's Jan."

"Oh, you are an absolute angel for calling me back. An *angel*. Margaret is sick, and Josh has *soccer* and he doesn't know *when* he'll get home, *plus* I swore to him that I would *not* use him as a live-in baby-sitter when he moved back. Mark and I have tickets to see *Phèdre*, and I *hate* the idea of giving them up. They're *sort* of a birthday present, which I say *not* to influence you in *any* way, because if you *can't* do it—"

"It's no problem," I said. "I'm free." *Plus I think I might be falling in love with your son.*

"Oh, you are *really* too good. Really. I'm *thrilled. Can* you come at six? We have six-thirty dinner reservations. If that's no good, I can *cancel* them with no—"

"Six is fine. I'll see you then."

"Terrific! Why don't you come over *early* so I can hear all about your life. I *miss* you." She whispered the next part. "Margaret's a *very* nice sitter, but she's just so *boring.*"

I promised to get there before six, and we got off the phone.

With only forty-nine hours to put together an outfit that said both "I am a responsible baby-sitter who will not abandon your child to pursue pleasures of the flesh" and "I am a sexual dynamo," I headed upstairs to evaluate my options. I tried on every single thing in my closet before settling on a see-through white shirt with a white tank top under it, and a stretchy red skirt. True, Sarah might be a little surprised if I showed up to baby-sit her daughter dressed like a hooker, but there was no reason not to push the envelope. Looking at myself in the mirror, I decided I had achieved the perfect balance of responsible citizenship and sizzling passion.

Plus, the ensemble did an excellent job of hiding my butt, which is my worst feature.

I called Rebecca to inform her of the latest developments, fashion and otherwise.

"No," she said when I described what I was wearing.

"But it's perfect." I could hear techno throbbing in the background. "Where are you?"

"Barneys." Barneys is a department store on Madison Avenue so chic it makes Bloomingdale's look like a Wal-Mart. "My mom's going through one of her I'm-a-terrible-mother crises, so she gave me credit carte blanche."

The unfairness of life will never cease to amaze me. "God, I hate my parents," I said.

"Listen to me. You have to de-emphasize your sexuality Friday night. Wait, hold on. . . . Do you have a liner with a little more brown in it?"

In my next life, I'm coming back as Rebecca.

"HELLO!" I shouted. There was no answer. "Hello! I realize I'm not the *Chic* fashion editor, but do you think I could have a minute of your precious It Girl time?"

"Sorry." There was a pause during which I could practically hear Rebecca looking at herself in the mirror. "Look," she said finally, "obviously you should do what you want, but I think you're taking the wrong approach. The last thing you want to do is be too sexy. You'll scare him off. You want to look pretty but subtle. . . . No, I think that's a little *too* brown."

I looked at my see-through shirt in the mirror.

"Now, when you say *subtle* . . ."

"You need to trust me on this: pretty but not too sexy, then you wow him with your witty banter. . . . That's perfect. I'll take that and the lipstick."

The see-through shirt looked really nice. And I couldn't help wanting to show off my little bit of tan left over from the summer. "Can't I wow him with my uncanny impersonation of a scantily clad high-school senior?"

"Try your low riders and the white agnès b. T-shirt."

"I'll call you back."

I took off what I was wearing and pulled on the jeans and the T-shirt. I stared at myself in the mirror. Rebecca was right about it being a good combination. Plus the white of the shirt did wonders for the waning-tan situation. I called her back.

"Well?" Techno had been replaced by the ambient noise of Fifth Avenue at rush hour.

"I take back everything I said. You are a genius."

"I know, I know. Sometimes I amaze even myself."

I turned my back to the mirror and looked over my shoulder. "These are extremely butt minimizing. Plus, I have this whole outdoorsy thing going on. It's like I just stepped out of a J. Crew catalog. Very Seattle."

"That's what I pictured."

Neither of us had actually ever been to Seattle, but we read a lot of magazines. I took off the jeans so I wouldn't stretch them out before Friday night.

"I can't believe I'm going over there," I said, collapsing onto my bed. "Do you think something will happen?"

Rebecca knew there was only one acceptable answer to my question, and so she gave it. "Definitely."

After we hung up, I lay there looking at the jeans hanging over the back of my chair and thinking about how cute Josh is. Then I started thinking about how cute Tom is. Then I started thinking about how crazy it would be if both Tom *and* Josh were into me.

REPORTER: So, Jan, tell your fellow Lawrence Academy students what it's like to have *two* incredibly hot guys fall in love with you. Were you surprised when Josh confessed his feelings?

JAN: *(Laughing confidently.)* Well, I think it was pretty obvious what was going to happen. I mean, *hello!* You don't have to be a mathematician to figure out that perfect outfit plus witty banter equals totally irresistible.

But you know, I really should not have given that interview (even if it was only in my head). Because in tenth-grade English we read this play called *Oedipus*, which is about how it's a big mistake to get too high on yourself. According to the ancient Greeks, when you get too cocky, it's because you suffer from something called "hubris." And when you suffer from hubris, the only cure is for the gods to take a few minutes off from drinking ambrosia on Mount Olympus, swoop down to earth, and ruin your life.

Which is what was about to happen to me.

In, ironically enough, English class.

CHAPTER TWO

"Can we please not talk about this right now? Because he's going to pass by here as soon as he's done in there, and I really don't want to be talking about him when he does."

"He can't *hear* us," Rebecca pointed out. "He's on the other side of the street."

"He'll sense that we're talking about him," I said. "People can sense these things."

It was the period after English, and we were sitting outside at Antonio's. Even though I was feeling way too horrified by what had just happened to eat, my story didn't seem to be having much effect on Rebecca's appetite. She had already doused her second slice with Parmesan, cut it up into bite-size pieces, and eaten the cheese and mushrooms off each square. Now she was rolling the dough into little tubes, lining them up, and popping them in her mouth.

"I still don't think I'm picturing it right. Did you, like, do this?" Rebecca pursed her lips and made a kissing sound.

"We're not best friends anymore," I said. "It's official. I hate you."

She laughed and blew me a kiss.

"I think I was suffering from temporary insanity," I

said, trying not to look across the street to the deli Josh had entered a few minutes ago.

"*Temporary* insanity?" Rebecca asked. She rolled another square into a tube and took a bite out of it.

I ignored her. "Obviously I'll be leaving New York and relocating to a small town in the Midwest, where I'll live out my life under an assumed identity."

"Obviously," Rebecca said. "I'm just glad we could share one last meal before you go."

I was only half listening to her. "It was just so *intense*," I said, staring at the door of the deli in spite of myself.

"Jan, it was *English* class. How intense could it have been?"

Just as she said that, Josh came out of the deli holding a paper bag, and before I could avert my eyes so it wouldn't be completely obvious I'd been staring, he saw me, smiled, and kind of half waved. Then he stood where he was for a minute, as if he was trying to decide something, and crossed over to us. Just for the record, Josh has an extremely sexy walk. It's like he knows where he's going, but isn't in any rush to get there.

"Hey," he said when he got to our table. He nodded at Rebecca and then me. He was wearing a green T-shirt and jeans that, unlike the jeans of most guys at Lawrence Academy, weren't ten sizes too big for him. I tried not to notice how perfect his body was.

"Hey," I said. My greeting might have sounded breezier if I hadn't choked on the "ey" part.

"Did you check out those essay questions yet?" he asked me.

"Kind of," I said. I was looking at a spot just beyond his shoulder rather than directly at him, as if the BROOKLYN'S FINEST FOTO sign was so fascinating, I couldn't take my eyes off it.

"Kind of?" he asked. He shifted his backpack higher up on his shoulder and I got a great view of his hands. The fingernails were square and very clean. I looked back at the BROOKLYN FOTO sign.

"I mean, not really," I said. Josh stood there, like he was waiting for me to say something. I, too, was waiting for me to say something, but the only words materializing in my brain were *Pictures in 1 hour or your money back*.

"Hey," he said after a minute, "I heard you're baby-sitting Hannah tomorrow night."

"Yeah," I said. There was a long pause.

"Well," he said finally. "See you around."

"Yeah," I said again. Rebecca was staring at me like I had two heads, something that might have enabled me to think of a better parting line than the one I finally came up with. "See you around."

"Wow," said Rebecca. "Your rapid-fire wit was so dexterous I could barely follow it."

"I want to die," I said, watching Josh's retreating back. "I want to be dead."

"Maybe you *are* dead," Rebecca suggested. "You *seemed* dead."

I was still watching Josh, who was getting smaller and smaller in the distance.

"This is not my fault," I said.

"Of course it's not." Rebecca sprinkled some Parmesan on her plate and pressed her finger into it.

"I know we used to think Mr. Kryle was all that, but I lay the blame for what just happened entirely at his feet," I said, shaking some ice cubes into my mouth.

Rebecca licked the cheese off her finger, which she then pointed at me. "Remember, there's always Tom Richmond."

"It's too late for that," I said. "I can't live in the past."

"*You can't live in the past?* Jan, yesterday you couldn't shut up about him and his stupid baseball cap," she said.

"That was then," I said, swallowing the last of the ice. "This is now."

Only that morning Mr. Kryle had been my favorite teacher and English my favorite subject, especially since we had just finished reading *Romeo and Juliet*, which, only that morning, had been my favorite play.

English stopped being my favorite subject, Mr. Kryle stopped being my favorite teacher, and *Romeo and Juliet* stopped being my favorite play at approximately 10:56 A.M. eastern standard time, which is when Mr. Kryle ruined my life by calling me up to the front of the room to act out the last scene in the play, the one where Romeo finds Juliet sleeping in the tomb and thinks she's dead.

Normally, I hate when English teachers make me act something out, but this morning I was in such a good mood thinking about how funny and cute Tom Richmond had just been in history that I didn't even mind when Mr. Kryle cast me as Juliet. Plus my part wasn't exactly demanding, considering all I had to do was lie down on Mr. Kryle's desk and pretend to be dead.

Plus, he cast Josh as Romeo.

As I lay down, folded my hands over my chest, and closed my eyes, I was thinking how ironic it was that the *very day* after Sarah asked me to baby-sit Hannah, her son and I were acting out one of the most famous love scenes in the history of the world. I mean, could the foreshadowing of our upcoming romantic evening have been any *more* obvious?

Then Josh started Romeo's speech, " 'O my love! My wife!/Death, that hath sucked the honey of thy breath,/Hath had no power yet upon thy beauty.' " He read his lines perfectly; suddenly nobody was talking or joking around like we usually do when people act out scenes. When Romeo described Juliet's "crimson" lips and cheeks, Josh touched my lips and my cheeks very gently, and it made my skin tingle. At one point, he even twirled a piece of my hair around his fingers, and then he tucked it behind my ear. I had expected to lie there trying to decide who I liked better, Josh or Tom, but once Josh touched my face, I couldn't concentrate on anything except what he was doing. Then I noticed how good he smelled, like shampoo.

At the end of the speech, Romeo's supposed to kiss Juliet. He drinks the poison, says, " 'Thus with a kiss I die,' " kisses her, and collapses. I heard Josh make a noise like he was drinking from a bottle, and then he slipped his arm under my back and lifted my shoulders off the desk.

Now, in my limited experience, when a guy puts his arm around you, like at the movies or something, either he barely touches you or he grabs you so tightly he cuts off the circulation in your arm. Neither one is exactly the sexiest sensation in the world. But somehow, Josh managed to hold me firmly without squeezing me so hard I couldn't breathe. He sort of tucked me against him, too, so along with his shampoo I could smell his skin, which also smelled really nice. My forehead was against his chest, and I could feel his heart beating. I waited for him to say his last line.

But he didn't say it. I waited what felt like five minutes, and then I opened my eyes a tiny bit to see what he was doing. He was just looking at me and holding me against him, and then he took my left hand and linked his fingers through mine. And the whole time he kept staring at my face, like he was trying to memorize it. I was afraid he would see my eyes were open, so I shut them. But he still didn't say his line. He just waited.

Which is when the *true* irony of the situation was revealed.

Because I actually thought he was getting ready to kiss me.

I have no excuse for this except the possibility that, as I told Rebecca, I may have experienced temporary insanity. I mean, I've been at Lawrence Academy since I was four, and not once in all those years have two students, acting out a scene in English class, ever actually kissed.

Kids barely kiss in the school *plays*. They've actually *rehearsed* kissing, and they still can't do it.

But there was something about how intensely Josh was looking at me, how he was practically cradling my head in his arms, that just made me think, *Oh, he's going to kiss me now*. I even, and I guess this is really the most awful part, I even sort of opened my lips a little and lifted my head a tiny bit to *get ready to kiss him back*. And that's what I was doing when he said his line and Mr. Jenkins and the whole class started applauding and the scene was over. Josh, who clearly had never had any intention of kissing me, let go, and then we both took these mock bows and shook hands, and the whole time I was thinking the same thing:

Did he see what I just did?

Which is why I not only need to change English classes but must enroll in the government's witness protection plan immediately.

Rebecca finished eating and dabbed at the corners of her lips with her napkin. If I even drink a glass of water when I'm wearing lipstick, it gets so smeared that I end up looking like a victim on *Law & Order*. Whereas Rebecca can consume a five-course meal and not even need to reapply her lip liner. When we go out and Rebecca has on a hot outfit and perfectly applied makeup, I'm pretty sure people assume she's my baby-sitter.

"I have to get back," I said. "I need to work on my Barnard application." Stepping out from under the awning into the sun, I felt as if the temperature went up about twenty degrees, which is just not a good thing if you have hair like mine. Last year in art history we saw slides of the Great Pyramid at Giza, and there is no way around the fact that that is exactly what my hair looks like on a humid day. Rebecca put on her sunglasses and waited while I rooted around in my bag for something to prevent my head from becoming a day in the life of ancient Egypt.

"You're not going to Barnard. You can't go to college in New York when you've spent your entire life here," said Rebecca. "You need to get out in the world. Experience other places."

"You wouldn't happen to have any particular place in mind, would you?" I asked. I found a stretched-out rubber band and gathered my hair into a ponytail.

"Why, Jan Miller, *whatever* could you mean?" We headed toward school.

"Oh, I don't know. Maybe you were thinking of . . . Providence."

"Hey, now that you mention it, Providence *is* a great town." Rebecca just happens to be applying early to Brown.

"So I've been told," I said.

At the corner of Clinton Street, Rebecca grabbed my arm. "Wait a minute. Don't you have French now?"

"I 'have' French in the sense that I am scheduled to be there," I said. "I do not 'have' it in the sense that due to a pressing obligation, I will be unable to attend."

"So you're cutting French to work on your application," said Rebecca.

"Precisely." French class is so humiliating, I'll take any excuse I can think of not to go. I know almost no French, but each year I do just well enough on the final to advance to the next level, thereby ensuring yet another year of misery. Every day is exactly the same. I walk in; the teacher greets me with a big smile; she says, *"Bonjour, Jan"*; I say, *"Bonjour, Madame"*; and it's downhill from there. Each time she calls on me I stammer out some totally wrong answer that has nothing to do with whatever she's asked, until finally, she gives up completely and ignores me for the rest of the period, which is pretty much a huge relief for everyone.

Right outside of school we ran into Richie, who's also in my French class. Richie lived in Paris for a year when he was in junior high, so it's a complete joke that we're supposedly at the same level. He's helped me a lot over the years, but lately even Richie has stopped promising me that "anyone can learn French."

"Tu vas au cours de Français?" he asked.

"I have no idea what you just said, but I'm not going to French." Richie was too nice to say anything, but I feel like everyone must be pretty relieved when I don't show up to class. It's like, hey, now we can actually learn a foreign language.

"Do you want me to call you about the homework later?"

"Not especially."

"Aren't you going to take French in college?" asked Richie. He tried to sound neutral, but I think I heard concern in his voice.

"Richie, my friend, after June twelfth, you won't so much as catch me sipping a glass of Perrier."

"Well, maybe that's for the best." He turned to head to class. "Hey, do you know that new guy, Josh?" he asked over his shoulder.

Sometimes when I'm nervous or embarrassed my face gets kind of flushed, and I was pretty much sure that was happening now.

"Ah, kind of. He's in my English class."

Rebecca snickered and then patted Richie on the shoulder.

"Well, Cupid," she said, "I gotta dash." She waved good-bye to me. "Call me later."

Richie shrugged as if to indicate that he had never had any idea what girls were talking about and didn't see any reason to try and figure it out at this point.

"He's in my math class," he said. He didn't seem to notice I was having a mild heart attack. "I think I'll invite him for next Saturday. He seems cool." Richie was having a party the weekend after next because his parents were going out of town. Even though Rebecca and I had sworn not to go to any high-school parties now that we were seniors, we were making an exception for his.

"Uh, I think he is," I said. "I mean, I think he's, you know, cool." Richie was already walking into the building. "I mean, I don't know him that well," I shouted at his back.

"Okay," he called over his shoulder.

"Well, I gotta go," I yelled at him. Considering Richie was already inside the building, it wasn't exactly clear why I was telling him this.

I didn't hear what Richie said as he disappeared, but it sounded like, *"Bonne chance."*

"Ha ha," I yelled back, even though he was gone.

Then I headed over to the computer lab, trying not to think about all the insanely dumb things I had said and done in the last two hours.

CHAPTER THREE

I could hear Mandy Johnson giggling even before I walked into English class the next morning. Rebecca and I were standing in the hallway right outside the door, trying to decide where to meet for lunch, when all of a sudden there was this squeal from inside the room. Literally a squeal. Like the violent death of some animal. Rebecca mouthed, "Nice laugh," and headed to her English class on the third floor.

After all that squealing I wasn't exactly surprised to find Mandy sitting on Josh's desk when I walked into the room; the only thing that surprised me was that she wasn't sitting in his *lap*, which was obviously where she wanted to be.

I must have dropped my backpack onto the desk a little harder than I meant to because it made a terrifically loud thump, and Josh looked up at me. I had planned on saying something casual yet significant about my babysitting Hannah, like, "Hey, catch you later," or maybe, "I guess you were wrong about spending Friday nights all alone," but instead I just looked away. Apparently people who say opportunity only knocks once know what they're talking about.

Mr. Kryle walked in just as the second bell was ringing,

looking, as usual, like he'd slept in his clothes the night before. Mandy miraculously managed to find the inner fortitude to peel herself away from Josh and go back to her seat. She was wearing tight capri pants and a tiny tank top, and she twitched her skinny little Mandy butt all the way over to her desk. In spite of my repeating *Please trip please trip please trip* over and over again in my head, she made it safely across the room and slithered into her chair.

"Hi, everyone," said Mr. Kryle, taking some books out of his briefcase.

We all kind of grunted hello, except Mandy, who said, "Hi, Mr. Kryle," in her cheeriest *Entertainment Tonight* voice. Do teachers actually fall for that crap? *Hi, Mr. Kryle! Have a great weekend, Mr. Kryle! I like your tie, Mr. Kryle. That was a very interesting reading assignment, Mr. Kryle.*

"So, let's talk about the essay." Everyone groaned. "Well, if no one wants to talk about the essay, I could always hand out *The Sound and the Fury* and give you a nice, fat reading assignment for tomorrow."

"Oh, can we please talk about the essay?" asked Mark Jacobs, folding his hands together like he was begging.

"Why, Mark," said Mr. Kryle in a chirpy voice, "what an excellent idea. I'm so glad you suggested it." He looked around the room. "Who's started working on the essay?"

"I *thought* about it," said Mark. "Does that count?" Everyone laughed except Mandy. She squealed.

"Well, I'd say that's about as good a place as any to

start. An essay of a thousand words begins with a single thought. Anyone else find yourself *thinking* about the essay?"

Mandy raised her hand, and Mr. Kryle called on her. Before she answered, she flipped her bangs out of her eyes and said, "Well," in this really dramatic way. I imagined pulling her frosted blond hair out strand by strand. Would her squeals of pain sound more or less like a dying animal than her laugh? I thought about what she would look like bald.

". . . which is why I like that, Mandy," said Mr. Kryle. I had been so busy imagining the look on Mandy's face the first time she was forced to confront her bare, red scalp, I had completely missed what she said. When Mr. Kryle complimented her, she looked over at Josh, but Josh was looking at Mr. Kryle.

"Any other ideas?" He looked around the room. I thought he hesitated when he got to me, but I pretended to be studying the cover of my book extremely carefully. After all, he was the one who'd gotten me into this mess. Lorrie Narkin, whose wardrobe this year consists entirely of clothing that has the word HARVARD stenciled on it, raised her hand, and Mr. Kryle called on her. I looked up and saw Josh looking over in my direction. For a second my heart started to beat faster, but then I remembered there's a clock right above my seat.

The Gardners live only about five blocks away from me, so I was a little early. Hannah answered the door, and as I stepped inside she threw her arms around my legs and started singing a little song that just went, "Jan Jan Jan. Jan Jan Jan." It was pretty cute, and it made me feel bad for how annoyed I get whenever she wants to play.

"I'll be ready in a second," Sarah called down. "I made a *tragic* fashion decision about fifteen minutes ago."

Hannah took me into the kitchen, where she was finishing her dinner, and started telling me all about the class rabbit. The house didn't look different even though Josh was living there now. There was a new DVD player in the living room that might have been his, but maybe they'd gotten it before he came. It had been a while since I'd baby-sat Hannah.

"Finally." It was Sarah.

When I was little and read books like *Peter Pan*, where the mother is described as sweeping into a room on a cloud of perfume and ermine, I never knew what it meant. My mom doesn't wear perfume, and even though I don't know exactly what ermine is, I'm pretty sure she doesn't have any. But the real reason I couldn't picture what the author was describing was because I couldn't exactly see my mom *sweeping* anywhere—she's more likely to clomp than sweep. But when Sarah walked into the kitchen and said, *"Finally,"* there could be no doubt this was exactly how Mrs. Darling *swept* into the nursery to kiss the children good-bye before *sweeping* off to some fancy London party.

"Mommy, you look pretty," said Hannah. And she did. Sarah was wearing a silky gray top and dark blue pants that flared at the bottom.

"Thanks, sweetie. Mommy's still recovering from an

earlier incident with Anne Klein separates." I told her she looked pretty, too.

"So *tell* me about *school* this year. Is the whole college application thing just absolute *hell*?"

"Pretty much."

"Details, *please*." She started transferring stuff from a big black bag to a small beaded clutch the same color as her top.

"Well, for one thing, the guidance counselors tell you to be creative and to try to express what makes you a unique applicant, but they don't really mean it."

"How so?"

"Like, there was this question on one application, 'What would be on page 275 of your autobiography?' So I wrote it as if I were this really dumb woman whose only claim to fame was having a series of famous men as lovers and husbands. It was all"—I adopted a breathy, slightly accented voice—"'After the devastating collapse of my third marriage, I escaped the fishbowl of Manhattan to recuperate in solitude at my snug little hideaway in the south of France, where Carlos and I had enjoyed such wonderful times together.' But my guidance counselor totally vetoed it."

Sarah was laughing. "Why?"

"He kept saying the essay had to show something about who I *really* want to be and how there's clever and then there's *too* clever. He wants me to write it like I discover a cure for cancer or something equally cheesy."

"But then *you'll* sound like all the *other* applicants."

"Tell me about it," I said.

"How about Josh? How does he seem to be doing? *Whenever* I ask it's always, *'Oh, Mom.'*"

"Um, he seems to be doing okay. I think he's, you know, making friends and stuff." Actually, I didn't really know if Josh was making friends, but I figured he probably was, since Richie wanted to invite him to his party.

"Well, maybe *you* two will be friends."

"Maybe," I said. I was glad she picked that moment to check her lipstick in the mirror so she couldn't see I was blushing.

When Sarah left, Hannah and I went up to her room to play. She wasn't that into playing with Barbie anymore—she wanted to play school. She was the teacher and I was the student, and I kept doing bad things and getting in trouble. Every time she said, "Go to Miss Kay's office!" (Miss Kay is the head of the elementary school at Lawrence), she would laugh until she practically fell over. By the time she had to go to bed, I'd been sent to Miss Kay's office roughly fifty times.

Once Hannah was asleep, I wasn't sure what to do with myself. It was only about nine, and I knew Sarah wouldn't be home until at least eleven. I figured there was no way Josh wouldn't be home before then. I kept calculating what time he'd get home if he'd just gone to practice, what time he'd get home if he'd gone to practice and then out for dinner with the team, what time he'd get home if he'd had a game and not a practice. No matter how generous I was in my calculations, I was sure he'd be home by ten. Which left me at least another hour with nothing to do.

The Gardners have cable and we don't, so normally when I baby-sit, I channel surf until I find some stupid movie I would never bother to rent or go to. Only tonight I wasn't exactly dying for Josh to come home and find me fixated on the climactic scene in *Save the Last Dance*. I considered watching a sporting event because it seemed like he was really into sports, but Rebecca would kill me if I pretended to care about soccer or basketball just to get some stupid guy to like me. Our utter lack of athletic ability was one of the things we first bonded over when we became friends back in the second grade. Plus what would I do if Josh asked, like, what my favorite team is? I practically haven't heard of any team except the Knicks, and I always confuse them with the Nets anyway.

I decided I'd do homework, since school was something we had in common. I could see it now:

(Sound of keys. Front door opens. Josh enters.)
JAN: *(Looks up from the book she is carefully studying.)* Josh, I didn't know you'd be home so early.
JOSH: *(Puts down his bag.)* I raced home as fast as I could. I had to see you.
JAN: *(Confused, but slowly understanding.)* You mean . . .
JOSH: *(Walking over and taking her in his arms.)* Yes, my darling. I can't stay silent any longer. I love you. I've loved you from the moment I first laid eyes on you. And now I must make you my own. . . . *(They embrace.)*

CURTAIN

It's embarrassing that my romantic fantasies are more soap opera than Shakespeare but, sadly, not as embarrassing as what actually ended up happening, which is that I fell asleep. And I don't mean curled up on the couch with a slim volume of poetry in my hand looking cute and soft like a Katie Holmes character. No, I mean sitting at the kitchen table with my head on my calculus textbook, drooling onto the page like Homer Simpson.

It went like this.

Having carefully put myself where Josh would have to see me when he came home—in the kitchen—I started doing my math homework. At first I kept thinking I heard someone coming down the block or fiddling for a set of keys. I was completely alert. I had put some lipstick on, and I was being careful not to smudge it. I was even sitting up extremely straight so my chest stuck out a little. In addition, I was armed with numerous funny, flirtatious conversation openers that I kept running over in my head so I wouldn't forget them.

As it got later, I started to slouch. Slowly, calculus worked its soporific magic, aided by the grandfather clock in the hallway ticking out, *You are getting sleepy. Very sleepy. Your eyes are getting heavy. They are closing.*

The next thing I knew, someone was touching my shoulder really gently and going, "Jan. Jan." And to kick off my campaign of seduction, I responded to his touch by batting his hand away, and then—just to make the moment absolutely perfect—I snorted.

Please do not let this be happening. Please do not let this be happening. I shook my head in a doomed attempt to clear my brain and rubbed my face where it hurt from falling asleep right on the edge of the book. I could feel a deep crease running across the middle of my cheek.

"Hey," said Josh. He went over to the fridge. "You want some water or anything?"

"Um, yeah. Thanks. What time is it?" *Do not panic. Do not panic.*

"Almost eleven."

"Oh. Really." He brought me a glass of water. *Wake up! Wake up! Say something!* "How was practice?"

"Actually, we had a game."

"Oh. How was that?"

He rummaged around in one of the cabinets, took out a bag of pretzels, grabbed a handful, and came over to sit in the chair next to mine.

"We won."

"Great." Even when I'm not half asleep, I have no idea how to talk about sports. Like, are you supposed to ask what the score was, or is that bad in case they only won by a little bit? "I guess you must be pretty psyched."

"Actually, I kind of wish the season would end already." He popped a pretzel in his mouth. "Last season I was really into playing, but now—I don't know. I'm kind of over it." *This is good. He's opening up about his feelings. Encourage more of the same.*

I racked my brain for a sports-related question.

"Was your team in Seattle good?" He was wearing a Lawrence Academy sweatshirt and a pair of Lawrence Academy shorts. When he'd leaned over to pour my water, I'd noticed he smelled really good again, not like shampoo, but like outside, like fall. His hair was all messy, and there was some dirt on his cheek.

"It was all right." He smiled his slow smile at me. "How was your nap? You were pretty out of it, there." He reached over and kind of tousled my hair.

Miraculously, I did not respond to his touch by fainting. "Yeah, well." Was that all I could come up with? *Yeah, well. YEAH, WELL?* This was not the witty banter required to supplement my casual, outdoorsy look.

"Don't feel too bad—I've had the same problem with calculus myself." Josh got up and went over to the counter. "You want some pretzels?" He took another handful.

"No thanks." I could just see myself trying to talk and spraying him with a mouthful of pretzel crumbs.

He brought the water pitcher over to the table and refilled his glass. "So," he said, sitting back down, this time across the table from me, "here we are."

I nodded. "Yup, here we are." This was not witty banter—it was an echo.

"What's the deal with Richie's party next Saturday," he asked finally. "Are you going?"

"Yeah, I'll probably go." We looked at each other across the table. His eyes were enormous, and they were very dark green. *Please please please please understand that I am not just deaf-mute-pseudo-nature-girl. Please.*

He smiled at me. "I'll probably go, too."

Here it was. Our big scene.

JOSH: *(Reaching across the table and taking Jan's hand in his.)* I'll probably go because I love you, Jan. *(They stare meaningfully into each other's eyes and then—)*

"Hello? Anybody home?" It was Sarah. Josh looked up as she came into the kitchen.

CURTAIN

CHAPTER FOUR

I wasn't exactly devastated when Sarah called me on Monday and said that Margaret, her regular sitter, had mono. Actually, whatever the opposite of devastated is, I was that. Sarah must have gone on for about a hundred hours saying if I ever *did* have a free Friday or Saturday night, she wanted me to know she was *dying* to hire me. I told her I could baby-sit again next Friday and she practically had a stroke thanking me.

I kept thinking of Friday as a date with Josh, even though Rebecca was kind enough to remind me about ten million times that baby-sitting a six-year-old is not the same as having a date with the six-year-old's seventeen-year-old brother.

"Can I just point out that less than a month ago you didn't even notice Josh?" We were sitting on the broken-down sofa in the corner of the student lounge, which was empty except for us and some freshmen huddled together way on the other side of the room. Every once in a while one of them would look nervously in our direction, like at any second we might invoke some secret senior privilege and order them to leave immediately. Little did they know: we seniors are far too busy tormenting ourselves to bother humiliating underclassmen.

"I noticed him a month ago," I said, avoiding looking at her.

"Yeah, you noticed him enough to think he was a loser."

"I know. I *know*." Just thinking about having said that made me drop my head onto my knees in humiliation. "I can't explain it."

"Don't feel bad," said Rebecca, patting me on the back. "You're just a fool in love."

I still had my head against my knees. "Why is this happening to me? Why can't I go back to the simple days of my youth when I liked Tom and everything was so clear?"

"You mean last week?"

"Exactly." I lifted my head and looked at her. "How am I going to survive until Friday?"

"Well," said Rebecca. "Look on the bright side. Maybe he won't even be there." The bell rang, and she stood up. "Why hire you if he's home on a Friday night?"

"*Because*. She doesn't want him to feel like he's the default baby-sitter." Students started swarming into the room, so I had to raise my voice to be heard. "She wants him to be free to come and go as he pleases."

"The key word there is *go*," said Rebecca, grabbing her backpack and swinging it onto her shoulder. And then we both broke out laughing, thinking about what the *other* key word was.

On Friday, while I would be on my not-exactly-but-almost-hot date, Rebecca would be stuck at home with her parents, who hate each other. Rebecca has no idea why they're still married. Her dad is a famous lawyer—sometimes he's even on the news and in magazines—who works constantly, and her mom is a movie agent who's always flying off to L.A., where most of her clients are. It's because of all the people her mom knows that Rebecca ended up being in *Chic*.

Every few months they have a really fancy dinner and make Rebecca sit through about ten thousand courses with all the incredibly boring people they know. Rebecca can usually snag a new outfit out of the occasion if she's in the mood, and last time she convinced her mom it was okay if she got this really sexy dress. All night her father's colleagues were telling her how grown up she looked and asking her to give them a hug. It was completely gross.

As soon as Hannah opened the door and saw me, she went running into the kitchen screaming, "She's here! She's here! She's here!" Then she ran back and grabbed my legs and made me walk with her standing on my feet.

"I have *two* baby-sitters tonight," she announced.

"You do?" I tried to sound interested yet casual, when really I was just interested.

Sarah was in this very pretty dress with a flower pattern on it and very high strappy shoes. "I'm running *so-o* late. Mark is going to *kill* me. But listen, you know where everything is, and Josh *should* be home in a little while." She kissed Hannah on both cheeks. "Good-bye, angel. Don't stay up later than nine." She looked at me. "There are *rewards* for you in the next life for *rescuing* me. We'll be home by midnight, but call my cell if you need *anything*." Then she waved at us and swept out the door.

"Are you the boss of me tonight or is Josh?" We went into the kitchen, where Hannah's dinner was partly eaten.

"Why don't you think of Josh as the CEO and me as chairman of the board?" Hannah looked confused, but I was too busy trying to decide if Sarah had meant Josh would be home soon and would then go out again, or if he would be home soon for good, to explain myself.

We were about halfway through *The Little Mermaid* when Josh came in. He was in his soccer uniform again and looked, if it was possible, even cuter than he had the week before. His hair needed to be cut, and after he put his soccer bag down he brushed his bangs out of his eyes with this totally sexy gesture that he didn't seem to realize was sexy. Hannah jumped off the couch and threw her arms around him, and he gave her this big, loud kiss on her cheek.

"Now you kiss Jan," she said.

"Yes, ma'am," he said.

I felt the beginnings of a panic attack.

JOSH: *(Putting Hannah down and taking Jan in his arms.)* Jan, I've wanted to do this for as long as I can remember.

JAN: *(Embarrassed.)* Oh, Josh, we mustn't. Not in front of Hannah!

JOSH: I can't help myself. I love you, my darling! *(He kisses Jan passionately.)*

CURTAIN

Josh came over to where I was sitting on the couch and, still holding Hannah, kissed me lightly on the cheek.

"EEEEWWWW!" Hannah shouted. Then she started singing, "Josh and Jan sitting in a tree, K-I-S-S-I-N-G!" I couldn't believe that song was still around.

"Very original," said Josh.

"Yeah," I added. "I don't think I've ever heard that one before."

"We're watching *The Little Mermaid*," Hannah informed Josh. "It's my twenty-fifth time watching it. Do you want to watch with us?"

"I think I'll pass. I need a shower."

I tried not to look disappointed. I also tried not to look like I was picturing Josh taking a shower.

Josh put Hannah down and she snuggled up next to me. "I'll see you in a bit," he said to me. And he smiled that smile.

I had never thought of *The Little Mermaid* as a particularly long movie, but suddenly every scene seemed to last forever. I heard Josh taking a shower, and then music came from downstairs, nothing I recognized. When Hannah made me rewind "Kiss the Girl" so she could see it again, I almost strangled her.

I was sure it was one in the morning when the movie finally ended, but it was only nine-twelve. In spite of my hoping Hannah would insist Josh come up to kiss her good night, she just yelled, " 'Night, Josh!' " downstairs and he yelled, " 'Night, Hannah!" back. I figured I probably shouldn't complain, since I did owe her for that first kiss, and I couldn't exactly expect a six-year-old to make all the moves for me.

The house was really quiet when I came downstairs, except for Josh's music coming from his room. I put Hannah's dishes in the dishwasher and straightened up the couch, and then there wasn't really anything left for me to do.

I couldn't decide what to make of Josh's saying, "I'll see you in a bit." Did he mean, *I'll come upstairs when the movie is over?* Did he mean, *You should come downstairs after the movie?* Did he mean, *I'll see you in class on Monday?* The last one seemed unlikely. Objectively, Friday to Monday is not "a bit." It's a few days. If he'd meant, *I'll see you Monday*, he would have said, *I'll see you Monday*. Of course, he could have meant, *I'll see you at Richie's party tomorrow*, but even that seemed like stretching the definition of "a bit." I wished I could call Rebecca, but she was probably only on her fiftieth course, too busy listening to gross middle-aged men say, "My, what a low neckline you have," to help me.

I was channel surfing and debating the ethical implications of going to the head of the basement stairs and shouting down, "Hey, do you know what channel the game's on?" when I heard him coming up. I tried to look like I was fascinated by what was on the TV.

"I wouldn't have pegged you for a NASCAR fan," said Josh, coming up behind me.

"What?" I craned my neck around to look at him. His hair was wet, and he was wearing a pair of jeans and a T-shirt that said PIKE'S MARKET: GET 'EM WHILE THEY'RE

FRESH on the front. He looked extremely clean and shiny.

"NASCAR racing. Do you like it?" He pointed at the screen, where some guy in a puffy suit was being interviewed next to what looked like a giant Matchbox car.

"Oh. Not really." There was a pause. "I think it's important to be well-rounded."

"Oh." We looked at the screen for a minute.

"I'm kidding," I said finally.

"Right." He walked toward the kitchen. "You want some ice cream?"

"Um, no thanks." I couldn't decide if I should change the channel or leave it where it was.

"Okay," he said. I decided to put on MTV, which seemed like a neutral choice. You can't really argue with MTV.

"You're not much of a talker, are you?" he called from the kitchen. "I mean, you're kind of quiet."

I had never hated anyone as much as I hated Mr. Kryle at that moment. "I'm not quiet. I'm, like, the *opposite* of quiet," I said. I could hear him taking out a bowl and rummaging around the fridge.

"You mean 'noisy'?" He came back holding two bowls of ice cream.

"Yes," I said. "Noisy."

He flopped down at the other end of the couch and handed me a bowl. "I thought you might have changed your mind about the ice cream."

"In thirty seconds?"

"Well, you know how girls are. If you don't want it, I'll eat it." He crossed his legs Indian style. "So, what's the deal?

I see you talking to your friend—what's her name? Rebecca?"

I nodded, amazed that any guy would refer to Rebecca as "What's her name."

"Is she the only one you're 'noisy' around?"

"Well, I mean, I don't know you that well yet." I couldn't decide if the *yet* was too forward. Maybe I should have left it out. Then again, if I hadn't said "yet," he could think I didn't want to *get* to know him. Maybe it was *good* that I'd said "yet."

Who knew flirting could be more complex than charting the course of U.S. foreign policy?

Josh, blissfully oblivious to the frantic negotiations going on in my brain, nodded and took a bite of ice cream. "You should ask Hannah. She's an expert on me. She'll tell you anything you want to know." He really had a great smile.

"Like what?"

"You'll have to ask Hannah. I wouldn't want to speak for her."

"Oh." I looked at the bowl of ice cream. It was some kind of chocolate with nuts in it. I hate nuts. "Well, maybe *you* could tell me something about yourself," I said, pushing at one of the scoops with my spoon and trying to see if there was a bite without any nuts in it.

He opened his eyes wide as if he were shocked by what I'd just said. "Now, that's a bold suggestion."

I adopted a mock-serious tone. "Here at Chez Gardner, we dare to be different."

"So you must be looking for a somewhat *daring* answer?"

"Well, if you're feeling *daring*."

"*Dare* I say, a radical answer?"

"I *dare* you." I located a small corner of a scoop that looked nut-free and ate it. After all, *Cosmo* says guys don't like girls who don't eat. Of course, guys probably don't like girls with butts the size of SUVs, either.

"Fascinating. Fascinating." He took another bite of his ice cream. "Something radical about myself."

"That's right."

"Completely unexpected."

"Exactly."

He didn't say anything for a minute. I tried to send him some suggestions via telepathy. *I hate Mandy Johnson. You are the most beautiful girl I have ever seen in my life and I love you.*

"Well," he said finally, "I'm kind of shy."

I want you to be my girlfriend. I've wanted to kiss you from the first second I saw you. You complete me. It took me a minute to realize he had actually said something.

"You mean you're too shy to tell me something about yourself?"

"No, I mean that's the thing about myself that I'm telling you. I'm kind of shy."

"Oh," I said. Could I work with this? Was he trying to tell me he was too shy to reveal his true feelings about me? Was his statement merely a confession, *or might it be a desperate cry for help?*

He stretched out his leg a little bit so that his foot was resting on my knee. My whole leg started tingling like it had fallen asleep. "So," he said. "Now it's your turn."

"I didn't know we were taking turns." Suddenly my hands felt sweaty.

"Sure, that's how it goes. I tell you something about me, you tell me something about you. That's what we in Seattle call *conversation*."

"Wow, you guys on the West Coast are pretty cutting edge." I wondered if it was possible to sweat so much that you raise the general humidity in the room and cause your own hair to frizz.

"Well, we try."

What could I say? I mean, given what he had said, this was clearly not the time to announce, *I want to marry you and have your children.* I needed to buy some time.

"Now, are you looking for something most people don't know about me, or can it be something most people already know but you don't?" *I hate tomato sauce. Jennifer Aniston is my favorite actress. I hope you don't mind that I have a butt the size of Central Park.*

"That's totally up to you." His foot was still on my knee. I started worrying my leg actually *had* fallen asleep. I wanted to move it, but I was afraid if I did he would take his foot away. I wiggled my toes just to make sure I could.

Why couldn't I think of anything? *English used to be my favorite subject. I'm allergic to strawberries. My parents won't get me a cell phone.* Was I the most boring person in the entire universe? Was there nothing I had to reveal to the cutest boy in the world?

"I hate the word *moist*." *Did I just say that? Please let me not have just said that.*

"Really?" Josh put his empty bowl on the coffee table and leaned back against the arm of the couch, lacing his fingers behind his head.

For a minute nobody said anything.

"I hate the word *ointment*," he said finally.

"Oh God, *ointment*'s the worst." I wanted to lean against the arm of the couch, too, but I was still afraid if I moved he would take his foot off my knee.

"How do you feel about *slacks*?" I asked. I settled for leaning against the back of the couch and turning my neck so I could still look at him.

"You mean the thing or the word?"

"The word."

"I'd have to say I'm against it."

"Ditto." We sat there for a minute, smiling at each other. My neck was starting to cramp, but I didn't move. There was no doubt this night was going to land me either in a relationship or a wheelchair.

The phone rang.

"Hang on a sec," said Josh. He walked around the back of the couch and touched the top of my head as he passed. My scalp tingled. I felt like the lady on the T-Gel commercial.

"Hello? . . . Oh, hey!" His voice sounded different all of a sudden, like he needed to clear his throat. "Um, can you, uh, hang on a second?"

He came back into the living room. I tried to look like I'd been focusing on the TV and not what he was saying.

"Listen," he said, holding his hand over the mouthpiece, "it's for me."

"Oh, right," I said. "Sure." I reached for the remote control.

"So, uh, I guess I'll see you at Richie's?" He held the phone in both hands up by his shoulder and rocked from one leg to the other.

"Right," I said again. We stayed there holding our respective electronic devices.

"Well, okay, then," he said.

"Okay, then," I repeated.

He swung the receiver around like it was a baseball bat. "See ya."

I angled the remote control toward him. "See ya."

He turned around and put the phone back up to his ear. As he walked away, he said, "Nothing, just hanging out," before closing the basement door behind him.

CHAPTER FIVE

I woke up on Saturday much later than I usually do. Even before I opened my eyes, I was thinking about Josh. If I concentrated really hard on my knee, I could still feel the spot where his foot had been.

Unfortunately, my room is about the worst place on the planet to analyze a complex romantic entanglement, since it was furnished when I was in third grade and in the midst of a bizarre identification with G.I. Joe. I chose a gray metal army-cot–style bed and a gray metal desk and an olive green rug that looks like AstroTurf. I still can't believe my parents indulged the whole quasi-military theme, what with their being all "No bomb-pops" and everything, but my dad says I threw such a major fit every time he tried to even hint that maybe someday I wouldn't want my room to look like a barracks, they let me do what I wanted.

(I would like to note for the record that the fit I threw last fall, when they wouldn't let me buy a pair of three-hundred-dollar Italian leather boots from Barneys, was not nearly as successful as the fit I apparently threw when my parents tried to convince me to sleep on a canopy bed instead of an aluminum cot. What did my eight-year-old self know that my sixteen-year-old self did not?)

I couldn't possibly be expected to make sense of the previous night all alone at Fort Miller, so I threw on sweatpants and went downstairs to get a fortifying breakfast before calling Rebecca.

My mom and dad had already finished eating and were sitting in the living room, reading the *Times*.

"How was baby-sitting?" my dad asked.

"It was fine. Nothing special."

My mom looked up from the paper. Since it was absolutely crucial that I get into the kitchen, make breakfast, and return to my room without getting into a discussion about (a) Josh or (b) the status of my college application pile, her look was a very bad sign.

My mom and dad both think it's important to express an interest in their children's lives. It's completely annoying. However, I have learned that when you are trying to keep from discussing *one* topic with your parents, the trick is not to say *nothing* because that makes them suspicious. What you need to do is introduce a *different* topic, ideally one so boring they will do whatever is necessary to put an end to the conversation. Normally I have a few of those topics on hand, but thinking about my phone call had left me vulnerable to attack.

I improvised. "We watched *The Little Mermaid*. It's really quite a sophisticated movie when you think about it."

"Oh?" my mom asked, smiling at me.

"Do you remember the scene where you first see Ariel's cave with all the stuff she's taken from the land world?"

"Not really." I saw her eyes dart over to the Metro

section. My dad wasn't even pretending to pay attention to what I was saying.

"Well, how about that song they sing to try and convince her life's terrible on land? You know that one?" I sang the first line from "Under the Sea."

My mom shook her head. She lifted the paper up a few inches so it half blocked her view of me. "Anyway," she said. "I'm glad you had a nice time."

Mission accomplished.

My dad always gets up early on Saturday mornings and buys delicious breakfast stuff like coffee cake and muffins and brioche even though he complains they're very non-Jewish food items. My dad is obsessed with what is Jewish and what isn't, which is kind of bizarre, considering we never go to temple or anything. He says he's a cultural Jew, and if someone asks what he means, he says he's not a Jew, he's Jew-*ish*. Then he cracks up.

This is only one of ten thousand things he does to irritate me.

I had just finished heating the milk for hot chocolate and was pouring it into my favorite mug, which, ironically, has all these French words and phrases written on it, when the phone rang.

"Are you alone?" It was Rebecca.

The downstairs of our brownstone is basically a big open area that includes the kitchen, the living room, and what I guess you could call the dining area. I leaned over the counter and checked out what my parents were doing; they seemed pretty engrossed in the paper.

"Um, kind of," I said.

"Okay, get alone and call me back." I took my plate with the coffee cake and my hot chocolate and headed to my room.

"Was that Twiggy?" My dad calls Rebecca Twiggy because according to him she looks just like this model named Twiggy from the 1960s. As you can imagine, there's really nothing better than having a skinny best friend who looks like a famous model when your butt belongs in *The Guinness Book of World Records*.

"But of course," I said.

"She should come for dinner soon," said my dad. "I feel like we haven't seen her in ages. How is she?"

I had one foot on the stairs. "I'm about to find out," I said.

"Remember when we were young and things happened to us?" my mom asked my dad.

"Vaguely," said my dad.

"See ya," I said, going upstairs.

I heard my mom sigh and say, "Youth," right before I shut my door, drowning out the parental nostalgia fest.

"It's me." I was sitting on the floor, leaning against my bed. I took a bite of coffee cake.

"I fooled around with a guy who works with my dad."

I always thought it was an exaggeration when characters in books or movies start choking after they hear a piece of shocking news, but the second she said the word *dad*, I felt a piece of coffee cake go down the wrong way, and I started to gag. She literally had to wait five minutes while I coughed and gasped, trying to catch my breath.

"Are you, like, hacking up a lung or something?" Rebecca finally said.

"What happened?" I managed to squeak out.

"Well, he's this guy who—"

"No, start with the first second of last night. Start with when you were getting dressed."

Rebecca told me everything from the beginning.

The guests at Rebecca's parents' dinner parties are always lawyers her dad works with and people her mom says are *incredibly* important in the movie industry even though we've never heard of them. She says they're the people who *really* make movies, which I guess means I'd rather have dinner with the people who *don't* really make movies, like Julia Roberts and Josh Hartnett.

Usually Rebecca's parents make a big deal about introducing her to each of the guests as they arrive and being all, "This is our *lovely* daughter," which makes Rebecca want to puke, but last night Rebecca was still getting dressed when people started arriving. By the time she was ready, her parents were each involved in intense conversations and barely saw her come down, so she kind of floated around the room, drinking champagne and avoiding talking to anyone. She ended up standing by the bar checking out the guests, and she kept making eye contact with this youngish guy who was talking to some older guy. The young guy kept looking over at Rebecca, and Rebecca kept looking over at him, and she kind of smiled, and he kind of smiled, and finally he said something to the older guy and came over to where Rebecca was standing.

"I'd heard the Larkins leave nothing to chance, but I didn't realize they hire people just to stand around looking gorgeous," the young guy said. Rebecca was wearing an extremely short strapless blue dress.

"Is that what I'm doing?" asked Rebecca.

"More or less," he said. Rebecca didn't say anything for a minute, and then he said, "Are you a lawyer? Are you standing there thinking about suing me for sexual harassment?"

"Not exactly," said Rebecca. She'd been trying to decide whether it was fair not to tell this guy she was his host's daughter. "I'm Rebecca."

His name was Brian and he was in his second year at Columbia Law School. He'd been a summer associate at Rebecca's dad's firm, and he was planning on working there full time after he graduated. Rebecca did the math and figured even if he'd gone directly from college to law school, he had to be at least twenty-two.

He asked what she did and she said, "Oh, you don't want to mix business with pleasure, do you?" and so he said, "You're right. Let's just keep this pleasure," and they kept flirting like that until Rebecca's mom announced that it was time to go in for dinner. So right as they were walking into the dining room, Rebecca's dad came over and clapped Brian on the back and put his arm around Rebecca and said, "Glad my daughter's taking such good care of you."

Rebecca said it was like something out of a sitcom. Brian practically spilled his drink on himself. He started calling her dad "sir," and saying things like, "You certainly have a very intelligent daughter, sir." Rebecca said nothing.

Rebecca and Brian were seated next to each other at dinner, probably because they were pretty much the only people there under a hundred years old. Brian was now completely ignoring Rebecca even though she kept trying to talk to him, and finally he turned to her and in this semisarcastic voice said, "You don't like to mix business with pleasure?"

So she said, "I'm really sorry about that."

"Were you planning to tell me who you were before or after I made a pass at you?"

"Were you going to make a pass at me?"

The whole time they were having this conversation, they were speaking really quietly and kind of fake smiling at each other so anyone who looked over at them would think they were just talking about something innocent, like the weather. By the time the sorbet came, their fight had taken on this whole flirtatious element, and he was like, "How old are you anyway?" and then, rather than say how old she really is, which is eighteen, Rebecca said, "I'm twelve." So then he said, "So you're in, what, seventh grade?" And she said, "Close, sixth." And he said, "What *are* sixth graders interested in nowadays?" and she said, "Oh, kids today are very advanced," and he said, "In what subjects?" and she said, "You know, math, science, dating." And he said, "Really, what does a sixth grader do on a date?" And she said, "We enjoy martinis at The Madison," which is this incredibly chic bar in Midtown where Rebecca and I used to go sophomore year because fancy places never ask you for ID. I guess they figure if you can pay the bill, you're old enough to drink there.

By this time they had both had a lot to drink and were basically ignoring everyone else at the table. I cannot imagine what my mom and dad would do if they had a party at which I spent the entire night alone in conversation with a twenty-two-year-old single man. Last year my dad had a dinner for the students in his graduate seminar, and one of the guys and I talked alone together in the kitchen for about 3.5 seconds. That night my dad came into my room after everyone left and asked if I'd been uncomfortable or anything when the guy and I were talking, and I was like, *Dad, give me a break, we were talking about garbage disposals.* Which we actually were! My dad said he was relieved, and then he gave me this whole speech about how I was becoming a very attractive young woman, and I might not realize it, and blah blah blah blah.

In other words, not only did my parents provide me with the enormous-butt gene, they are clearly determined to ensure that any man who miraculously manages to overlook my freakish figure will never get to be alone with me long enough to ask me out.

So the dinner was winding down, and everyone was going out onto the terrace for coffee and dessert. Brian and Rebecca got up and went outside with all the other guests, and then Rebecca said, "Do you want to see the Empire State Building?" And he said, "Can you really see the Empire State Building from here?" and she said, "Well, we have to go to the other side of the apartment," which is true since they were on the side facing south and the Empire State Building is to the north. She didn't know if he knew what she was planning, but he followed her around the corner, away from all the other guests and up these stairs to the terrace that's off her bedroom.

The Empire State Building was orange, and they tried to decide if that was in honor of Halloween or Thanksgiving. Brian asked if she'd gone trick or treating, and they started joking about how she had gone as Britney Spears with all her little friends. And then she said, "Do you think Britney Spears is sexy?" and he said he hadn't really thought about it, and she said, "Don't you kind of want to kiss her?" and he said something like, "As an attorney I have some concerns about the legality of all this," and then they kissed.

"OH MY GOD!" I said.

"I know," she said.

"Who kissed first?"

She thought about it for a second. "I want to say it was him, but objectively I think even at the last second he was kind of hesitant. I mean, once we started, it was definitely mutual, but I had to push it along."

"How far did you go?"

"We just made out. But my God, Jan, he is *such* a good kisser!"

"Did anyone notice you were gone?"

"It's possible, but I doubt it. He went back around the terrace, and I went through the apartment so it wouldn't seem too obvious."

"You are so cool," I said.

"I know," she said.

"So, are you going to see him again?" I was tracing my initials in the crumbs from the coffee cake.

"Well, when I said good-bye, I slipped him a note. My dad's going, 'We can't thank you enough for coming,' and all that crap and Brian's going, 'Oh, you have such a lovely daughter and such a lovely home—'"

"He *said that*? He *said*, 'lovely'?"

"Something like that. I mean, he was definitely all, 'Your daughter is such a sweet child,' and not, 'Thanks for having me, I had a great time feeling your daughter's ass on the terrace earlier.'"

"He felt your *ass*?"

"Well, he mostly had his hands on my back, but then a couple of times he was kind of grabbing at it."

"Was it weird?" I didn't think I would like having my butt grabbed. Of course, only King Kong has hands big enough to grab it, so the question is clearly moot.

"Actually, it was kind of cool." She paused for a second. "So don't you want to hear what the note said?"

"Oh, yeah. I totally forgot."

"It said, 'Meet me at The Madison next Friday at ten.'"

"Oh my God!" I jumped up and accidentally knocked over the last of my hot chocolate. "That is *so cool*."

"I know," said Rebecca. "Sometimes I amaze even myself."

"What if he has plans?"

"He'll have to break them."

Obviously there are about five million differences between me and Rebecca, but if I had to name the most crucial one, it would be my asking *What if he has plans?* and her saying, *He'll have to break them.* Even if I could imagine seducing someone who works with my dad, which I can't, and even if I had the guts to lure him up to our nonexistent terrace and start kissing him, which seems unlikely given my history of relying on a first grader to make the first move for me, and even if I could think of a cool thing to write like *Meet me at The Madison next Friday at ten*, I would never ever *ever* in a million years be cool enough to leave it at that. If I'd written that note, it would have said *Meet me at The Madison next Friday at ten, or, if that's no good, maybe you're free Saturday at ten. If you'd prefer to meet earlier in the evening, maybe around eight o'clock, that's okay, too. I realize it's also possible you're out of town next weekend, in which case the following weekend would be just fine.* Then it would have had nine million ways to reach me, including e-mail, telephone, mailing address, and emergency contact information.

Clearly this is one of the many things that separates an It Girl from a Not It Girl.

"So how was baby-sitting?"

"It was a disaster." I took a sock and mopped up most of the hot chocolate. The one advantage to my horrible rug is, it never stains.

"Barbie and Ken have a big fight?"

"Josh was there."

"He *was*? Tell me *everything*."

"I wish there was something to tell." Compared to hers, my night was suddenly even less *Sex and the*

City and more *7th Heaven* than it had been an hour ago.

When I got to the part about Josh sitting down with me on the couch, she said, "I thought you said there was nothing to tell."

"That's the thing—that's all that happened."

"What do you mean?"

I told her about the rest of the night.

"Bummer," she said.

"I know," I said.

"You should have just made the first move."

"You know, I thought about it, but I didn't want him to think I was retarded *and* sexually deviant."

"Making the first move does not equal sexual deviancy."

"Why is it that in the middle of a dinner party you can seduce a guy whose career could be destroyed for life if he gets caught with you, while I am incapable of leaving even the slightest impression on Josh? *Nothing, just hanging out.* That's a direct quote. I can hear it like it was yesterday."

"It *was* yesterday."

"You're hysterical."

"It doesn't mean anything that he said that. A person could say 'Nothing, just hanging out,' in response to a lot of questions besides 'What are you doing?'"

"Name one."

Rebecca didn't say anything for a minute. "Well, maybe he didn't want to *reveal* what he was doing. *Maybe* it was his girlfriend in Seattle, and he needs to break up with her so he can go out with you, only he doesn't want to make her suspicious, so he didn't want to say, 'I'm hanging out with this really hot girl.'"

"With the world's biggest butt."

"Would you please get over your butt, Jan?"

"Maybe I could if I was a pole vaulter."

"YAHN!"

"If he's going to break up with her, why did he spend the rest of the night on the phone?"

"Maybe he was breaking up with her *last night*! Maybe he was breaking up with her the whole time just so he could be free to ask you out at Richie's party."

I thought about it. "I want to believe you."

"I know."

"Yet I feel I must keep at least a minimal grip on reality."

"I wouldn't bother. Reality can be very upsetting." I had to agree with her there.

We decided Rebecca would come over to my house in time for us to arrive fashionably late at Richie's, even though I knew leaving from my house instead of hers could mean a major battle with my parents. They've always been vaguely suspicious of high-school parties, and now that I'm a senior they're completely convinced that every social gathering is destined to be a den of iniquity, complete with alcohol, illicit drugs, and sexually experienced guys eager to do unmentionable things to my body.

Here's hoping.

CHAPTER SIX

Even before I discovered Mandy and Josh alone in a dark corner at the back of Richie's garden, my night was teetering on the edge of disaster.

It all started a little before nine o'clock, which is when I suddenly discovered I had nothing to wear. I couldn't believe it, and neither could Rebecca, since she's always the one running around her room half dressed complaining that she hates all her clothes right when we're supposed to be walking out the door. In the history of our friendship I doubt if she has once waited for me to get ready.

But it turns out you don't need a walk-in closet the size of Texas to have a fashion crisis.

"What about jeans and a T-shirt?" Rebecca was being really patient, considering I'd insisted she get to my house by eight forty-five so we could leave at nine on the dot.

"I wore that baby-sitting. He might remember." I was standing in the middle of the room wearing the huge SLC Olympics 2002 T-shirt I sleep in.

"How about the skirt you were going to wear baby-sitting that I told you not to wear?"

"It's in the laundry."

She got up off my bed and started going through my

closet, something that takes about one minute from start to finish. "What about these?" She held up an old pair of cargo pants.

"Makes it look like my butt gave birth to a second butt." I sat down on the floor and pulled the neck of the T-shirt up over my head. Originally I had planned on wearing this really cute pale blue sundress, but all day the temperature had been dropping until it was way too cold for a little sundress no matter how cute it was. "This is so symbolic. Everything I plan is a disaster." I curled up on the floor, keeping my face hidden by my T-shirt. "If my life were a Broadway play, it wouldn't even make it to Broadway. It would close in New Haven."

"Don't panic," she said. She thought for a minute. "Okay, here's the plan. First: I smoke a cigarette. Second: we find something in this house that makes you look *totally* hot."

"You mean like a different body?"

"Ha ha, very funny, Yahn," Rebecca said.

I put on my dad's long parka over my shirt and listened while Rebecca, who was wearing a pair of tight black jeans and a stretchy black shirt, explained her theory that I was only fixating on what to wear because I was nervous about seeing Josh and was neurotically seeking to control a situation that was, by definition, beyond my control.

Sometimes it's helpful to have a best friend who took a psychology elective. Other times I wish she had signed up for photography instead.

I finally ended up in a pair of jeans and this really nice black cashmere sweater of my mom's. She used to be pretty cool about letting me borrow her clothes until last spring, when I spilled an entire can of Diet Coke on her brand-new suede jacket. Now I'm supposed to ask before I borrow something, but was it my fault if she and my dad were out for dinner, and I couldn't reach them because they refuse to embrace twenty-first-century telecommunication, i.e., the cell phone?

Even though I kept telling myself not to get my hopes up, the whole subway ride I couldn't help thinking about what Rebecca had said.

JOSH: Sorry I had to take that call last night, but I
 needed to break up with my girlfriend so I could
 tell you how I feel.
JAN: How do you feel?
JOSH: *(Taking her in his arms.)* I feel like this. *(Kisses
 her.)*

CURTAIN

By the time we got to Richie's block, my stomach was in knots. Life would be so much simpler if guys were like mood rings, and they changed color when they liked you.

"Jan, you have to slow down," said Rebecca. "This is not the fifty-yard dash."

She was right; I was practically sprinting. "Sorry."

Richie lives about five blocks from Lawrence Academy in this enormous townhouse. It's right on the promenade, which means spectacular views of the Brooklyn Bridge and Manhattan skyline—the perfect backdrop, in my humble opinion, for my big love scene with Josh.

We passed a group of people sitting out on the front steps, but Josh wasn't with them. He wasn't in the living room, either, where about ten people were standing around drinking beer. All I really wanted to do was find him, but racing around the house asking *Has anyone seen Josh? Has anyone seen Josh?* ran counter to the image of myself I wanted to project, so I calmly followed Rebecca into the kitchen.

As she grabbed us two beers from the fridge, I thought I got a glimpse of Tom Richmond heading down the back stairs. My heart started racing, and I quickly turned so I was facing away from the stairs—a girl, like an algebra problem, can only handle so many variables. The last thing I was equipped to do was talk to the person I used to like better than the person I now liked better than I liked him.

Just as I was worrying that Tom might recognize me from the back, Rebecca spotted Drew, Richie's brother who graduated last year. He was out back smoking with some other people from his class. She waved to him and he mouthed, "Come here!" so we went out on the deck. He gave Rebecca a big bear hug, and then he grabbed me and gave me a hug, too. And that's when I saw them. Mandy and Josh standing by a tree, T-A-L-K-I-N-G.

At first I wasn't even sure it was Josh, since it was pretty dark in that corner of the garden and his face was shadowed. But then he moved slightly, and I saw the sleeve of this fisherman's sweater he wears sometimes. He was facing the deck, and as soon as Drew let me go, I stepped to the side so I could see Josh but he couldn't see me.

Rebecca started asking Drew all about school, and soon

they were involved in this incredibly boring conversation about how great Brown is, and how much Rebecca wants to go there, and how if she gets in he'll show her around so that she won't waste the first few weeks hanging out with losers. I was pretending to follow their conversation, but really I was just watching Josh and Mandy.

Mandy was doing most of the talking. She was gesturing a lot and flipping her hair all over the place as per usual. I swear, someday she's going to give herself whiplash. Josh wasn't saying much, but he was listening intently, like he really cared about what she said. At one point she got him to stand up straight by kind of pulling him toward her; then she drew a line at about his chin to illustrate something. He kept nodding and nodding, and then she said something that made him burst out laughing.

Could *Mandy* be the reason Josh had broken up with his girlfriend last night?

JOSH: Mandy, I must tell you. Even though you laugh like a hyena, I love you.

MANDY: *(Laughing like a hyena.)* You do? *(Hair flipping ensues.)*

JOSH: Yes, Mandy. It is inexplicable, given that you are the stupidest slut in the universe, yet I cannot deny my feelings for you any longer. *(They embrace.)*

CURTAIN

Just as I turned my back to Josh and Mandy, a couple of junior girls came out on the deck and ran screaming at

Drew like he was the Bachelor. I thought I saw Josh look up when he heard them, but I couldn't tell if he saw me or not. Richie said something to the girls like, "How're my ladies doing tonight?" and Rebecca said, "Let's go in, I'm getting cold." I followed her.

More people had arrived while we were outside. Someone had put on an Ozomatli CD, and half a dozen people were sitting around the dining room table playing quarters. All the excitement I'd felt earlier was gone, and I was considering trying to convince Rebecca we should just go home and rent a Jennifer Aniston movie.

"I'm surprised Josh isn't here yet," said Rebecca. We were standing by the fridge drinking beer. There were at least twenty people in the kitchen, which was hot and crowded.

"He's here. He's in the garden."

"He *is*?" Rebecca looked confused. "I thought we were looking for him."

"He's talking to Mandy Johnson," I said.

"That *slut*," said Rebecca.

"You read my mind," I said.

"Well, this night is sucking just as much as we predicted," said Rebecca, holding her beer bottle up to mine. "Here's to no more high-school parties."

I clinked my bottle against hers. "I'll drink to that." Right as I took a swig of my beer, I saw Josh's sweater out of the corner of my eye. I half turned my back to the door and faced Rebecca.

"Incoming at two o'clock," she said.

"I saw him," I said. My head felt tingly, and I forced

myself to focus on the cabinets on the opposite wall of the kitchen.

"*Hey.*" It was Josh. He put his hand on my neck and gave it a mock shake. "Didn't you see me wave to you outside?"

I turned to him, trying to look surprised, which I was, a little. Rebecca said, "Hey, Josh," and he said, "Hey, Rebecca," and then she slipped away.

"No, I didn't," I said. I tried to think of something really clever to say, but apparently my brain had gone AWOL . . . again.

Josh looked at me kind of strangely, half frowning, half smiling. "Oh. Well. How are you? I was wondering where you were."

"Um, I'm okay." *Though I sure could use my brain right about now.* "How are you?"

Josh didn't answer my question. Instead he said, "I just found out the strangest thing. You know Mandy?" I tried to nod in a way that conveyed my familiarity with Mandy but not my desire to remove her eyes with my fingernails. "Well, it turns out her friend is this girl who went to my old school, you know, in Seattle?" I nodded again. "So this girl, her friend, is *incredibly* hot. I mean, every guy at my school wanted to go out with her, but she never went out with anyone. I mean, *never*. And a lot of guys tried, dozens. There were all these rumors about her, you know, that she had some boyfriend somewhere only he was a lot older or something, or that she was an ice princess. But it turns out . . . well, Mandy was just telling me, she's a *lesbian*!"

"No *way*," I said. Was there a chance Mandy was a lesbian, too? Suddenly the night had taken a one-hundred-and-eighty-degree turn.

"*Way,*" he said. "Mandy said they spent a summer at Bennington together and the whole time she was fooling around with a girl in Mandy's dorm!" This was not as good as if she'd been fooling around with Mandy, but it was better than if Josh had said, *Mandy was just telling me she's in love with me, which is a real coincidence because I'm in love with her, too.*

"Wow," I said. "Are you going to tell anyone?"

"No," he said. "I mean, it's tempting but . . ." He trailed off.

"But . . ." We were being wedged up against the wall by all the people crowding around us.

"But I think the kids at my old school are probably more prejudiced than kids at Lawrence. I mean, Mandy was cool about it, but I don't think the kids back there would be."

"That's funny," I said. "I always think of Seattle as being a really enlightened city." Actually what was funny was that I had just started a sentence with the phrase *I always think of Seattle as being* since I never actually think of Seattle at all.

"Yeah, I know what you mean," said Josh. "You just don't think of Starbucks and prejudice as going hand in hand."

"And Silicon Valley," I added.

"Actually, that's northern California," he said.

I laughed like he'd just said the funniest thing I'd ever heard. "Right. Sorry."

"Did you mean Microsoft?"

"Right. Microsoft." My voice had developed a metal-
lic ring, as if instead of being a girl at a party, I was in a
play where I had to *act* like I was a girl at a party. "I can
never keep all that stuff straight."

"Stuff?" asked Josh, smiling.

"You know. Technology. Geography. Stuff."

He laughed his awesome laugh. "If you live there it's
not hard to keep Microsoft straight. Basically it's like,
'Welcome to Seattle: brought to you by Microsoft.'"

I laughed, too, and brushed my hand over his wrist.
There was an article in, I think, *Glamour* that said men's
bodies immediately respond to a woman's touch by producing more endorphins or seratonins or something. It's
a subliminal seduction technique.

Josh didn't seem too affected by my touch, though.
Maybe the response is also subliminal.

"Is it strange for you being so far away from your cor-
porate sponsor?" I asked.

"Sure. But there's a chip in my head so they can keep
track of me at all times."

By now the kitchen had become so crowded we were
practically smushed up against each other.

"So you're saying Bill Gates might be listening to our
conversation right now?"

"Exactly," said Josh just as someone bumped into him
and he fell against me. I sucked in my stomach and stuck
out my boobs a little.

"Sorry to be practically on top of you," he said.

"Don't worry about it," I said. It was hard to speak

since I was holding in my abdominal muscles so tightly. Josh's face was very close to mine. Why did he always smell so good? Tonight in addition to his usual shampoo-Josh smell, he smelled slightly of the beer he'd been drinking. *Listen, I wanted to tell you that I broke up with my girlfriend last night. . . .*

"So, are you having fun yet?" he asked, smiling down at me. He had one hand up on the cabinets behind me, and he was holding his beer in the other. All I needed was about five more people to try and cram into the kitchen.

Someone squeezed in behind Josh, whose thigh pressed into mine. I started to answer him. "It's not too—"

"Hey, Jan!" I looked up in time to see Tom Richmond coming toward me. The crowd in the kitchen parted like he was Moses and they were the Red Sea. "How's it going?" he said when he got over to me. I shrugged, and he laughed and put his arms around me and gave me a hug. It wasn't a *bad* hug, but it was no *Romeo and Juliet* hug, either.

"Do you know . . ." I turned to where Josh had been a mere second ago, but he was gone.

"Do I know *what*?" he said in a voice that only a little while ago I would have found incredibly sexy.

My dad has this proverb he likes to repeat: *When the gods want to punish you, they answer your prayers.* In the case of Tom Richmond, the punishment is that they waited two weeks to give me an answer.

By then, the prayer had changed.

CHAPTER
SEVEN

"You've *got* to check this out," said Tom. He had his arm around my shoulders and was guiding me out of the kitchen and into the living room. I kept looking around for Josh, but it was as if he had disappeared into thin air. When we got to the foyer, Tom turned me toward the steps leading upstairs.

So many people were sitting on the staircase it was like an obstacle course, but once we got to the third floor there was no one around. Tom led me down a long corridor past several closed doors. At the end of the hall he stopped, turned to me, and said, "Ready?"

"Yeah, sure," I said. I had logged so many hours back in September imagining being alone with Tom, now that I actually *was* alone with him, I felt an uncanny sense of déjà vu.

"Check it out." He pushed open the door and pulled me in behind him.

We were in what I guess had once been Drew's room but was now more like a den with a lot of Drew's stuff all over the place. The lights were off, but the room wasn't dark; it was lit up by New York. The Brooklyn Bridge shimmered and was reflected in the black of the East

River, and as I got closer to the window, I thought I could make out people milling around the South Street Seaport. The view was so beautiful that for a minute I forgot to think about why Tom had been so eager to have me appreciate it. But as soon as I saw the Empire State Building, I knew he had taken a page straight out of Rebecca's book.

"Wow," I said. Why was it everyone but me knew how to use the beauty of the New York skyline as an instrument of seduction? Was I the only senior at Lawrence who lacked this skill? Had there been an assembly on it one day when I was absent?

"I'll show you *wow*," he said, putting his arm around my shoulders again.

And then Tom kissed me.

Or for accuracy's sake I should say, *attempted* to kiss me. Mostly he just started drooling onto my face and pushing me, as if I were his opponent in a wrestling match. I managed to partially resist his attempt to maneuver me onto Drew's bed, which resulted in our being half on the bed and half on the floor. At this point, Tom must have decided that this was as close as we were going to get to lying down because he stopped trying to get on top of me and started grabbing at my chest while licking my eyelid.

Ever since elementary school, I have been waiting to experience a good kiss, and all I can say is: I'm still waiting. In junior high I went to parties and played Spin the Bottle and Three Minutes in Heaven and Six Minutes in the Closet, and as far as I'm concerned, if some guy thrusting his slimy tongue in my mouth is heaven, send me to hell. I assumed things would get better in high school, but except for the bottle and the closet, it was just more of the same. Tom Richmond grabbing at my boobs like he was a passenger on the *Titanic* and I was the last remaining lifeboat gave me the feeling that senior year wasn't going to bring a big improvement on the status quo.

It was completely depressing because I had very high hopes. When I was eleven we rented a house on Fire Island for the summer, and the people who owned the place had left all these really cheesy romance novels behind, so I spent July and August reading books with titles like *The Promised Passion* and *The Lingering Longing*. They're basically how I got my idea of what sex was going to be like—you know, women being carried away by some guy touching their heaving bosoms. Even if my heart belonged to Josh, when Tom had leaned in to kiss me, I assumed I would have to struggle to resist the *tingling limpness running through my limbs*.

But it wasn't much of a struggle resisting the slippery strand of saliva running down my cheek.

The combination of drooling onto me and grabbing at my mom's cashmere sweater was clearly becoming too much for Tom, and he started breathing pretty fast. I, on the other hand, was barely breathing at all since the last thing I wanted was some errant strand of saliva to run up my nose and drown me.

The time had come to draw the line. Tom pushed my turtleneck aside and started half sucking, half nibbling on my neck while making a noise that sounded like, "Mooo." The door opened for a second and then someone shut it quickly, saying, "Oh, sorry." I decided this was my cue.

"Listen, Tom, I should probably go. It's getting late." Actually, I had no idea what time it was.

"You don't have to go," said Tom, licking my chin.

I resisted the urge to wipe my face. "Yeah, actually, my parents are *really strict*," I said.

"What time do you have to be home?"

"Um, what time is it now?"

Tom managed to check his watch while barely taking his lips off mine. "Eleven-thirty."

"Oh my God," I said, as if he'd just told me it was two A.M. Tom, unimpressed by my manufactured hysterics, jammed his fingers at my chest. Was this supposed to turn me on? Was this what caused bosoms to heave all over the world?

There actually *was* a part of me that wanted to heave, but it wasn't my bosom.

"Just stay a few more minutes," he said, pushing me back against the bed.

"No, really. I need to go. My parents will *kill me* if I'm late." It was as if in the few minutes we'd been making out, Tom had grown a dozen additional arms. Every time I managed to peel one of his hands off me, another one materialized on a different part of my body.

"What's their problem?" he panted. Or I think he did. It was hard to hear what he was saying since his tongue was licking my eardrum.

"Oh, they're *tough*." I mentally substituted Tony and Carmella Soprano for my art-history-professor father and documentary-filmmaker mother.

"That sucks," said Tom. He loosened his grip on me for a second, and I managed to shake myself loose and stand up. After a minute he did, too.

"Well, I . . ." he started to say. I could see him moving in for another grab and backed toward the door.

"Ah, good night," I said, putting my hand on the knob and turning it.

"Yeah, good night," he said as I opened the door. "We should try and—"

"Yeah, bye," I said. The only thing I wanted to try and do with Tom Richmond was avoid him, and that didn't seem like something we could really work on together.

Downstairs I searched for Rebecca, who was sitting next to Drew on the kitchen counter.

"I think I'm going to go," I told her.

"Where have you been? You've got—" She reached her hand out toward me.

"I'll call you tomorrow," I said, backing away.

"But—"

"I'll call you tomorrow."

As I walked over to Clinton Street to get a cab, my feet seemed to be beating out a rhythm that went *guys suck guys suck guys suck*. Slowly it evolved into *life sucks life sucks life sucks*. At Clinton Street there weren't any cabs, which is very unusual since there's usually one every minute or so. *Guys suck life sucks guys suck life sucks guys suck life sucks.*

What exactly are you supposed to do when a guy starts kissing you? There you are, having a nice time, minding your own business, just trying to appreciate a beautiful view, and the next thing you know someone's got his tongue up your nose. I mean, do I need to start carrying pepper spray?

"Life sucks!" I shouted out to the universe.

"Jan?" I turned around. *Oh my God. OH MY GOD! OHMYGODOHMYGODOHMYGOD!* There he stood. Tall. Beautiful. Perfect.

"Josh?"

"Hey," he said. "What's so sucky about life?" Wearing his black wool cap pulled down low on his forehead and a blue peacoat, Josh looked like a very cute sailor on shore leave.

"What?"

He repeated himself, carefully enunciating each word. "What. Is. So. Sucky. About. Life?"

I made a vague gesture as if to say, *Oh, you know. Poverty. Hunger. Racism. Bad kissers*, and then we just stood there for a minute. I hopped from one foot to the other.

"I was going to get a cab home," he said finally.

"I was going to get a cab home, too," I said.

"Maybe if we combine our efforts we'll have better luck," he said. He gave me a half smile, and I realized the rakish grin on Josh's face was probably the look Tom had been going for when he first slid his arm around my shoulders in the kitchen.

"Sure," I said. I put my arm out, thinking, *Stay away, cabs. Stay away, cabs.*

Of course an empty cab pulled up immediately.

"You seem to have the touch," said Josh as I opened the cab door.

"It's a native New Yorker thing," I said, sliding across the seat.

"Where to?" asked the driver.

We gave him our addresses.

"I thought you'd left," said Josh.

"Oh." What can you say to that? *Actually, I was upstairs being mauled by Tom Richmond.* "No, I was . . . still there."

"Oh."

Silence. Josh started tapping his knuckles against the window. *Tap.* Pause. *Tap tap.* Pause. *Tap tap tap tap tap.* The hand that wasn't tapping was on the seat mere centimeters from mine. I thought about Rebecca saying, *You should make the first move.* I willed my hand to drift over to his, but it refused to budge. *Move. Move.*

Nothing. Apparently having a crush turns you into a quadriplegic.

When the cab pulled up in front of my house, I reached for my wallet, but Josh said he'd pay.

"So," I said. I'd said it emphatically, like I had a really significant follow-up. Unfortunately, all I followed it up with was "Good night." I opened the cab door.

"Good night," he said.

Do not let me get out of this cab. "I'm glad I ran into you," I said.

"Yeah," he said. He was smiling at me in a way I couldn't quite identify. I could see the meter ticking out of the corner of my eye.

"That way we didn't each need to pay for a cab," I said.

"Yeah." He was still smiling.

"Well, I guess you're still paying for a cab, aren't you?"

"I guess I am," he said. In the light of the cab I could see his flawless skin, his beautiful green eyes. *I love you I love you I love you.*

"But we did save gas," I pointed out. "And that's good for . . . fuel emissions and, you know, the greenhouse effect." I was starting to sound like National Public Radio.

"True," he said.

"Well. Good night."

"Good night."

As I got ready for bed, I replayed the cab ride in my mind. Okay, true, we'd sat in complete silence for almost twenty minutes, but maybe that was a *good* thing. I mean, at least nothing hugely embarrassing had been said. Maybe he'd even start thinking I was a deep, introspective person, the kind who actually thinks before she speaks. While other girls were satisfied to string together banal observations along the lines of *What a great party!* and *This sure is some cold beer!* I felt no need to utter a word unless it was a pithy, insightful observation about the human condition.

When I went into the bathroom to wash my face,

things with Josh became clearer. Looking in the mirror I saw I had lipstick smeared across my chin. Running down the center of the smudge was a thin line where Tom's drool must have proved too strong for the staying power of Bobbi Brown.

CHAPTER
EIGHT

I don't know if it was the phone ringing or the yelling that actually woke me, but by the time I was fully conscious I could tell that (a) my mom was on the phone with my brother, (b) they were in the middle of a *major* fight, and (c) the only way I was going to get back to sleep was to go someplace quiet, like the runway at Kennedy airport. My mom's study is right above my room, so I could hear what she said whenever she raised her voice, which was most of the time. My dad was up there, too, on the extension in their room.

The first words I actually deciphered were, "I can't believe you would want to go to her house for Thanksgiving when you *something something something*." Then my dad said, "*Something* family *something*."

"A girlfriend is not *something something*. You have a *something something*." There was another pause, and he said, "I don't see how you call that an adult *something*."

Until he went to college, my brother and my parents always got along; by third grade I'd probably had more fights with them than he'd had all through high school. He was on the squash team at Lawrence, first JV and then varsity, so every day he pretty much just went to school, played squash, came home, and did his homework. He had a match or a tournament most weekends, and he wasn't around a lot. So I guess you could say their relationship was only as good as it was because he was never home, but that wouldn't account for how when he *was* home he didn't do stuff like leave his dirty clothes all over the place or forget to write down phone messages the way I apparently did.

Basically, he was the good child and I was the bad child, a duality confirmed by the fact that on the day he got accepted to Yale, my parents received a letter saying my French grade was "in danger of being compromised" by my "failure to attend class."

But then Rogier started Yale and got a girlfriend, and everything changed between him and my parents. As far as I know, Rogier never even kissed anyone in high school, but he was hot and heavy with this girl Heather from, like, day one of freshman orientation. They stayed together for the rest of the semester, but then in January he broke up with her and started going out with this *other* girl, Jamie or Julie or something.

None of us ever met the Julie person because before school ended he got a third girlfriend, Larissa. Over the summer, Larissa and Rogier came up to our house on Cape Cod, and one afternoon my mom *walked in on them by accident*. I don't know if she actually *saw* them, but either way, the entire thing is simply too gross for words. It turned into this gigantic fight, with my mom screaming at Rogier about how whenever he comes home he treats the family like he's a guest and we're the servants, and how he can't just do whatever he wants wherever he wants to. I was kind of psyched because that's the kind of stuff she's always yelling at me about. But *then* she started yelling at Rogier about how he has a little sister to think about, and how he can't behave around me the way he behaves around his college friends, and he said, "Well, Mom, she's hardly in kindergarten." So then my mom says, "I'm not saying she's in kindergarten, I'm just saying she doesn't have to feel pressured into doing things she's not ready for because she sees her big brother doing them!"

The only thing worse than having no sex life is having people scream at each other about your hypothetical sex life while you're in the next room listening.

I guess I should be glad Rogier's become such a Don Juan since it means there's hope that my sex life will improve next year. I definitely don't remember any girls at Lawrence ever liking him except for this one friend I had back in eighth grade named Tanya. She moved away sophomore year, but until then she was always asking me a million questions about Rogier and begging to come over to my house after school. Once when she was over, he came home from squash practice and walked from his room to the bathroom in a towel. I thought she was going to pass out.

"HELLO!" I shouted at the ceiling. "Some people are trying to get some SLEEP around here."

I pulled a pillow over my head and lay in bed replaying the end of last night. I started with when we were on Clinton Street and ended with closing the cab door, focusing exclusively on lighting. I was pretty sure it had been too dark for Josh to notice my lipsticked chin while we were out on the street, and during the actual ride it was pretty dark, too. That meant there were only a couple of brief minutes when he could possibly have seen that the bottom half of my face was dripping with saliva and Plum Berry! Objectively, how bad could it have been? Maybe he hadn't even noticed. I mean, everyone knows guys are completely oblivious to things like makeup and fashion. Maybe Josh just assumed I was experimenting with a new style: the Ringling Bros. and Barnum & Bailey Circus–gone-psycho look.

The door opened.

I lifted the pillow high enough to see my mom standing in the doorway in her green corduroys, a flannel shirt, and no makeup. Rebecca told me that in France, ancient secrets of fashion, perfume, skin care, and seduction are passed down from mothers to daughters. Looking at my mom, it was no surprise I was about as much of a femme fatale as Tinky Winky.

"Your dad and I are going into Manhattan. Do you want to come?"

I rolled over and pulled my pillow back onto my head. "Haven't you heard of knocking?" You'd think after what happened with Rogier this summer she wouldn't come near one of her kids' rooms without a written invitation.

"Look, Yahn, I'm sorry I forgot to knock. But it's not necessary for you to use that tone of voice with me."

"Well is it *necessary* for you to wake me at

dawn?" I took the pillow partway off my head, but I didn't turn toward her.

"Yahn, it's eleven-thirty!"

"Studies show teenagers need to sleep later than other people. It's in our BIORHYTHMS!"

"Nobody needs to sleep later than eleven-thirty." She was using her I-know-you-need-to-be-patient-with-teenagers-but-this-is-ridiculous voice.

I put the pillow back over my face. "Well, I'm sure the Nobel Prize committee will be thrilled to hear about your groundbreaking research on teenage sleep patterns."

She walked out and shut the door. I wanted to shout *No wonder Rogier wants to spend Thanksgiving with his girlfriend!* but I had the feeling she was in the mood to punish one of her children, and I didn't want it to be me.

I pulled the covers up to my chin and lay on my back, perfectly still, trying to go back to sleep, but every time I closed my eyes all I saw was a lipstick-covered chin floating against a dark background.

Eleven forty-five on a Sunday morning and nothing to do all day but contemplate suicide.

I called Rebecca's cell.

"Hey," she said, even before I said hello. "Why didn't you let me wipe that stuff off your chin last night?"

"I was experimenting with a new look," I said sarcastically.

"Were you upstairs fooling around with Josh?"

"Okay, I guess we can make it official: you have *no* future as a detective."

"Why are you pissed at *me*? I *tried* to warn you."

I told her about Tom and about taking the cab home with Josh.

"That blows," she said.

"Clearly. Do you think I should call him?"

"Tom?"

"Josh!"

"And say what, exactly?"

"Well, I was thinking I could call and ask him about the English homework and then slowly work the conversation around to how I'd probably had lipstick smudged on my chin when we were in the cab because I always try to rub my makeup off before I get home because my parents won't let me wear any since they're Amish."

"I really don't think you should say that," said Rebecca.

"But I don't want him to think my lipstick was smeared because I was fooling around with another guy. Then he'll never ask me out."

"But he's not asking you out anyway."

"Thank you *so much* for reminding me."

"Sorry. Listen, I have to go. My mom's pretending to care about my welfare, so we're having a day of beauty at Estée Lauder."

"When my mom wants to show me she cares about my welfare, she yells at me for not doing my college applications."

"Yeah, well. Some people have all the luck. I'll call you later."

"Bye."

I needed to stop thinking about last night. I needed to stop thinking, period. I hung up the phone and looked around my room for something to distract me. My backpack was crouched threateningly on my desk. There, a mere five feet away, lay hours and hours of distraction. I crawled to the edge of the bed, unzipped my bag, and got out *Romeo and Juliet* and the sheet with the essay questions. The second question was, "*Romeo and Juliet* is, in some ways, really a play about Juliet, who changes far more than Romeo does. Trace her evolution from child to adult over the course of the play." I had already decided to write on that one. Given my current situation, I couldn't help relating to a character whose love life gets so screwed up she fakes her own death.

The essay was due Monday, and I hadn't started it. I went back to the beginning of the play and started rereading scenes with Juliet in them, but returning to the scene of the original crime was not exactly getting my mind off Josh. Not to mention the fact that every time I blinked I was assaulted by the image of . . .

I *had* to focus on Shakespeare.

Good pilgrim, you do wrong your hand too much,
Which mannerly devotion shows in this;
For saints have hands that pilgrims' hands do touch,
And palm to palm is holy palmers' kiss. . . .

To call or not to call? Wrong play, right question.

Sophomore year Rebecca and I took a sociology elective called Gender Roles and Courtship Rituals. After reading about Aborigines in Australia and the Bushmen of the Kalahari, the class used magazines like *Cosmo* and *Maxim* to determine what rules govern modern American courtships. It didn't take long for us to conclude that the motto of the women's magazines is, *Let men pursue you or they'll think you're a desperate slut*, while the motto of men's magazines is, *Women who pursue men are desperate sluts*.

Twelve-thirty. Why shouldn't I call? Fact: Josh describes himself as "shy." Fact: I am not shy. Fact: If women ever hope to be liberated from the oppressive models provided by our misogynist culture, we must grab the mantle of power. I wasn't calling Josh for me, I was calling him for women everywhere. For our daughters and granddaughters. For our great-granddaughters. I picked up the phone, dialed, and hung up before it could ring.

I would never have a great-granddaughter. I would live with my parents until they died, and then I would grow old alone, wearing tacky, pseudo-vintage clothing and eating cat food. I could not seize the mantle of power. I could not even seize the training bra of power.

I considered sending Josh a message via telepathy until I remembered my recent use of extrasensory communication indicated the universe had gotten its wires crossed. Unless I wanted a call from Tom Richmond, I'd better not start trying to reach Josh via ESP.

I reopened Shakespeare.

O my love! My wife!
Death, that hath sucked the honey of thy breath
Hath had no power yet upon thy beauty.

I picked up the phone and dialed.

He answered on the first ring. "Hey. Sorry I couldn't talk before."

"Josh?" My voice was strangely high-pitched.

"Leslie?" *Leslie?* LESLIE? Who was Leslie?

"No, it's, um, Jan." My hand was sweating. The receiver slid around in my palm.

"Oh, sorry. I thought you were someone else."

"Leslie." I wedged the phone between my ear and my shoulder and wiped my hand on my comforter.

Josh laughed softly. "You're sharp." Actually, with my sweaty palms and complete lack of a reason for calling, sharp was pretty much the last thing I was feeling. Dull would have been a more accurate description. Dull and drippy.

"So, what's up?" he asked.

"Not much." Actually my heart rate was pretty "up." Maybe this could become a whole new way to burn calories: calling the guy you like for no reason at all. A few more minutes on the phone and I wasn't going to have to worry about my butt being too big anymore.

"What's up with you?" I asked after a pause. *Extremely original, Jan. Extremely.*

"Well, since you last saw me, I'd have to say zero," he said, laughing a little. His laugh sounded easy and natural, exactly the opposite of the forced giggle I responded with. "You know. Sleep. Shower. Breakfast."

"Same here," I said. "Well, except for the shower breakfast part."

"Sleep well?" asked Josh.

"Can't complain," I said.

There was a click.

"Hey, that's my call waiting. Can you hang on just a second?"

"Oh, yeah. Sure." I leaned back against the pillows. My hand wasn't sweating as much anymore. Actually, this conversation wasn't going so badly. A little chatting, a little banter. By now we were only about two innuendos away from a romantic comedy.

Josh clicked back.

"I gotta go. Were you calling for my mom?"

"*Yes!*" I said a little too loudly. I sat up. "I *was* calling for your mom. I was calling for your *mom*." There was a slight chance I might have been overdoing it a bit.

He waited a minute and then asked, "Um, anything in particular? Is it about Hannah? I think that Margaret person who usually baby-sits her is better."

"*What* a relief! Because the reason I was calling is I can't fill in for Margaret anymore. I have a thing next weekend and it's, um, just a big thing I can't get out of."

"No problem. She's not home now, but I'll tell her about your . . . thing." I wished I could tell if he was smiling or not.

"Great! I *really* appreciate it. Your telling your mom for me." Why couldn't I just stop myself?

"No problem. Well, I gotta get going."

"Leslie, right?" *Leslie? Are you kidding? Like I'd ever get off the phone with* you *for some person named Leslie. It's my dad calling collect from Tokyo.*

"Right."

"Okay. Well, bye." With the hand that wasn't holding the phone, I gave a little wave to the opposite wall.

"Bye."

I hung up, wondering if it was too late to drop out of Lawrence and get my GED.

CHAPTER
NINE

"Really, Jan. That's the grossest thing I ever heard."

We were trapped in the library because students weren't allowed to go off campus all week, a policy that might have had something to do with the fact that Rebecca and I weren't the only seniors who had been cutting class left and right.

"You don't know the half of it," I said. "He was just poking at my boobs the whole time like this." I used my index finger to poke at an imaginary breast.

"Why did you *let* him?"

"I don't know. I felt bad. He seemed so into it." Rebecca rolled her eyes.

"Well, what was I supposed to do, punch him?"

"Um, how about just saying no?"

"You're heartless."

"This is why you *have* to go out with older guys," Rebecca said for the millionth time. "Brian didn't poke me once. He really knows what he's doing."

"What about Mr. Just Touch It Once?" I pointed out.

"That was different." Rebecca looked annoyed. "He was a freak."

Rebecca's always saying how mature older guys are, but every time she and this "actor" she went out with last year fooled around, he would practically break her fingers trying to get her to put her hand down his pants. Then he'd go, "Just touch it once. Please, just touch it once."

"All I'm saying is you've fooled around with two older guys and one was a total pervert and one wasn't. Your set is too small for statistical accuracy."

"Who are you, Mr. Andrews?" Mr. Andrews had been our math teacher in ninth grade.

"Do you think Mr. Andrews ever asked anyone to touch it once?" I asked.

"Only if by 'it' you mean his pocket protector." Rebecca started laughing, and then I started laughing. Every time I tried to stop, I would picture Mr. Andrews begging someone to touch his pocket protector, and I'd lose it all over again.

The librarian, Mrs. Deaver, (or as we affectionately think of her, the Beaver), came marching over to us.

"Girls, you have had several warnings. I want you out of the library." We were laughing too hard to say anything, so we just grabbed our bags and ran into the hallway. Or Rebecca ran into the hallway. I ran into Josh.

"Easy there," he said as I banged into him. He held my shoulder as I took a step back. "You okay?" he asked.

My trajectory caused Rebecca to go into another round of hysterics. Luckily I, unlike her, am not the most immature person in the world and was therefore able to pull myself together.

"Sorry about that," I said, doing a fairly reasonable imitation of someone who was not dying of complete and utter embarrassment.

"It's a good thing I ran into you, actually," said Josh.

"Actually, I ran into you," I pointed out.

"Touché," he said, smiling. He was wearing a Wesleyan sweatshirt, and I made a mental note to work extra hard on my Wesleyan application. Perhaps we were destined to be thwarted during our senior year only to find true love there, in the romantic atmosphere of the small Middletown campus. I could see it perfectly.

Setting: *The registrar's office at Wesleyan.*
Scene: *The first day of freshman orientation.*

JOSH: Jan? *(His smile broadens when she turns around.)* I thought that might be you.

JAN: *(Smiling.)* Hey, Josh. *(Her hair is subdued in the low humidity of a fall day in Connecticut. Her miraculously tiny butt looks spectacular in a pair of tight jeans.)*

JOSH: I had no idea you were a student here.

JAN: Nor I you.

JOSH: *(Shyly.)* You know, last year I never had the chance to tell you how attractive I find you. *(He moves closer to take in the subtle fragrance of Jan's perfume.)*

JAN: *(Coyly.)* Well, I look forward to hearing all about it. *(Music swells.)*

CURTAIN

". . . would be a big help," Josh finished. "If you don't mind."

"No, I don't mind," I said. *Mind what? Mind what?* Whatever he said had been drowned out by my mental musical crescendo.

"Thanks a lot. I'll call you later."

"Right," I said, backing away from him without turning around.

"Watch the wall," he said, just as I banged right into it.

"Thanks," I said. "I'm kind of klutzy." As if my slamming into the wall two minutes after slamming into him didn't make that totally obvious.

"You probably shouldn't walk backward, then," he suggested.

"Good advice," I acknowledged. "I'll try and remember it."

"I'll call you later," he said, turning around and going into the library.

Rebecca was waiting for me on the stairs. "Josh is calling me later," I told her.

"Wow, that was fast. How do your Amish parents feel about your having a phone?"

"Ha ha. It just so happens he needs me to help him with something," I said.

"What?" The bell rang and students started pouring into the stairwell. I turned to go upstairs to history.

"I have absolutely no idea."

I waited as long as possible to go into the classroom since the last thing I wanted was to get there when an empty seat next to me might encourage Tom Richmond to sit in it. Naturally I was late, got yelled at by Ms. Smith, and then Tom wasn't even in class. Had he been hospitalized for dehydration after losing all that saliva Saturday night?

What had Josh asked me to help him with? What had I agreed to do for him? The possibilities were endless. *Would you tutor me in French? Would you help me with my Wesleyan application? Would you donate a kidney?* Yes. Yes. YES!

It was a C day, so English was last period. I waited for Josh to show up, and when he didn't, I couldn't help coming to a very depressing conclusion: Josh didn't need an ongoing tutorial. He didn't need a major organ donated.

He needed the English homework.

Still, I could work with this. I mean, okay, it was a banal, quotidian, pedestrian request (according to my SAT vocabulary flash cards), but it was a start. After all, he did not ask Mandy Johnson if he could call *her* for the homework. He did not say, "Mandy Johnson, put down your lip gloss and call me with the homework." No, he asked *me* for the homework. "Jan," he had said in his hour of need, "help me."

When I got home, my dad was in the kitchen, cooking dinner. He was wearing a plastic apron with all these different kinds of peppers on it and this chef's hat my mom gave him for his birthday last month.

He looked like an enormous mushroom.

My dad loves cooking. His dream is to open a restaurant somewhere out in the country. Personally, I don't see how anyone's dream could involve exposing himself to public ridicule, and when he asked me to set the table, I took our quality time together as an opportunity to mention this.

"I won't lie to you, Dad," I said, carrying the plates over to the table. "I don't think that chef's hat is working for you."

"I thought *Sixteen* said they're all the rage out in L.A.," he said, tasting something from one of the pots he'd been stirring.

Sometimes it's hard to tell if my dad is the most obtuse person in the world or if he's making a joke. "You do know it's *Seventeen*, right?" I asked.

"Taste this soup," he said. "It's like heaven on earth." He held out the spoon to me and I slurped at it. It was pretty good.

"Seriously, Dad. Chefs today are much more chic than they used to be. You don't have to look like the Pillsbury Doughboy to be a good cook." I took some silverware and went back to the table.

"It tastes great, doesn't it?" When my dad doesn't want to deal with whatever I'm saying, he just pretends I haven't said it.

"Yes, yes! It's great. You're the best chef on the planet. And you would still be the best chef on the planet if you didn't have that deflated pancake on your head."

"You know, honey," he said, walking over to the fridge and taking out a head of lettuce, "one of the pleasures of getting older is you stop obsessing about what other people think of how you look."

"I'm not talking about *obsessing*," I said. "I'm talking about a healthy awareness of other people's aesthetic needs." The phone rang.

"Hold that thought," said my dad, reaching for the phone. I forced myself to fold the last napkin really slowly and carefully, like I wasn't at all interested in who was calling.

"Phone's for you," he said, holding the receiver toward me.

I didn't want to talk to Josh—if it was Josh—in front of my dad. After all, there is simply no way to tell when a casual conversation about the English homework will evolve into a confession of true love. Unfortunately, I'm so superstitious that I was sure if I went upstairs to pick up the extension in my room before finding out who was calling, I would jinx it, and the call would turn out to be Rebecca or someone equally not Josh.

I took the phone from my dad, trying to tell from his expression who it was, but his face was perfectly blank.

"Hello?"

"Hey." It was Josh. My heart started to pound.

"Hey. Can you hang on a second?" I asked my dad to wait to hang up the phone for me and went upstairs. I picked up the phone in my room. "Got it!" I screamed.

"Okay," said my dad.

"Hi," I said.

"Hey. That your dad?"

"Yeah. He's making soup," I said, as if Josh would

be fascinated by my father's activity of the moment. I started folding and refolding a corner of my comforter, making it into a tiny triangle and then smoothing it out.

"Listen, thanks for getting the English homework. The coach pulled us all out of class for this unbelievably stupid meeting."

"No problem," I said. There was a pause.

"Ah, what is it?"

"Oh, right. We have to read the first fifteen pages of *The Sound and the Fury*," I said.

Josh laughed. "Well, I guess my not having the book is going to be a little bit of a problem, isn't it?"

Oh my God, why hadn't I thought of that? The book! The book!

The book!

"Well, you could just come over and borrow mine," I suggested casually. My heart was beating so fast I could barely talk.

"Hey, thanks. That would be great. It's due tomorrow?"

"Oh, no. Actually, not until Wednesday." My fast-beating heart slowed down considerably.

"Then I'll just go and get the book from Mr. Kryle tomorrow."

"Sure."

I was flat-lining.

"But thanks a lot anyway. Mr. Kryle got *so* pissed last time I missed an assignment because of soccer. I think he's kind of anti-sports, you know?"

"*Really?*" I attempted to sound shocked that *anyone* could be anti-sports.

"Yeah. I think a lot of people think athletics and stuff are a waste of time."

"They do?" I was trying to remember if the Nets were a New York team and, if so, what they played. Luckily, Sarah chose that moment to shout a question at Josh.

"Jan!" he shouted back to her.

I liked hearing him say my name.

Sarah said something I couldn't make out. "Oh, yeah," Josh answered. "Listen," he said to me. "I have kind of a weird favor to ask." *Will you be my girlfriend?*

"Shoot," I said casually. I wondered if he picked up on my subtle use of basketball terminology.

"Your dad's a professor at Columbia, right?"

"Right," I said.

"Okay, the thing is, I have this cousin who's applying to Columbia, and my mom was wondering if your dad would be willing to talk to him."

"About Columbia?" *Duh.*

"Yeah." Sarah yelled something else to Josh. "What?" he shouted. "Okay, I'll ask. My mom wants to know if you and your parents want to come over for dinner on Friday."

"To your house?" *Duh.*

"Yeah, so my cousin can talk to your dad and stuff."

"Um, sure." *Yes! YES! YES! YES! YES!* "I mean, I'll ask them."

"Well, okay. I guess I'll see you tomorrow."

"See you tomorrow."

"Bye."
"Bye."

When my father cooks Italian food, he likes to blast opera and sing along. If he doesn't know the real lyrics, he just makes them up. As I walked into the kitchen he was belting out, *"Oooh, my pants are in the oven!"* His chef's hat had fallen back on his head, and there were little bulges of fat hanging over the string of his plastic apron.

All my dreams of happiness depended on this man.

It was a terrifying thought.

CHAPTER TEN

"You didn't!"

"I did."

"Oh my God!"

"I know." It was Wednesday evening (or, as I preferred to think of it, T minus two days), and I was sprawled out on my parents' enormous king-size bed throwing Q-tips at Pieter, our cat, who likes to bat them under the rug. We'd already gone through most of the box.

"But what if he finds out?"

"How would he find out? He's not exactly about to call the dean of students and say, 'Hi, I'm a second-year law student, and I'm just trying to confirm that a young woman I met at a party and am romantically interested in is, in fact, a senior at New York University.'"

"Didn't he ask why you live at home?"

"I told him I couldn't deal with dorm living and my parents won't buy me my own apartment."

"So now instead of thinking you're in high school, he thinks you're a spoiled little rich girl."

"An *of-age* spoiled little rich girl. It's not my fault. I had every intention of telling the truth. I *told* him I was a senior, but then he said, 'In *high school*?' and he sounded so horrified I had to say college."

It's not like I'm morally opposed to lying about how old you are. I mean, Rebecca's not the only one with a fake ID burning a hole in her Kate Spade bag (well, I guess technically my fake ID is burning a hole in my *fake* Kate Spade bag). But it does seem to me there's a difference between flashing an Arizona driver's license at a bouncer and constructing a false identity in order to seduce one of your father's employees.

"So are you going to make up classes and a major and stuff?"

"I doubt it'll get that far. He kept saying he wasn't even going to show up."

"But you're going?"

"He'll be there."

"How do you know? He *said* he couldn't make it."

"He called, didn't he?"

"Maybe he's just a nice guy," I said. "He didn't want you waiting around for him, so he called to say he wasn't coming." Pieter was backing away from and then attacking the Q-tip lumps under the carpet. He takes the game very seriously.

"He left his *number*. He could have just said, 'Rebecca, it's Brian. I'm sorry, but I'm not going to meet you at The Madison on Friday.' Click. End of story. He didn't need to be all"—she made her voice deep and sexy—"'Hey, it's Brian. Why don't you give me a call on my cell?'"

Pieter looked up at me, and I threw him another Q-tip. He pounced on it. "How'd he get your number?"

"Information." She took a drag. "Plus, why the long

conversation? It takes ten seconds to tell someone you're not going to meet her somewhere. We were on the phone for half an hour. He'll be there."

Drinks at The Madison. Were there any circumstances that could possibly result in Josh and me being thrown together at The Madison's hip, sexy bar?

Setting: *A Midtown street during a sudden rainstorm. Jan is huddled under the awning of The Madison Hotel. Josh walks by her and then turns around.*

JOSH: *(Not sure if it's her.)* Jan?

JAN: *(Equally unsure.)* Josh?

JOSH: *(Smiling.)* It is you. What brings you here?

JAN: *(Tosses mane of thick, nonfrizzy hair over bare shoulder.)* I was just shopping for this backless evening gown I'm wearing. What about you?

JOSH: *(Reaching out to wipe an errant raindrop off Jan's cheek.)* I just finished soccer practice nearby. *(Waves vaguely.)*

JAN: What a coincidence.

JOSH: *(Looks up at the rain.)* You wouldn't by any chance be free for a drink, would you?

JAN: Actually, I would. But I don't think you can go into The Madison in your soccer uniform.

JOSH: Oh, I always bring a tuxedo with me wherever I go.

JAN: *(Noticing his garment bag.)* Well, then, let's have that drink.

JOSH: *(Smiling knowingly.)* I was hoping you'd say

that. *(He opens the door, revealing The Madison's dimly lit, sleekly modern bar, and holds it for her.)* You know, I've been thinking about you a lot lately. . . .

CURTAIN

"Hello? Hello! Earth to Jan. Come in, Jan."

"Sorry. I just can't believe that two nights from now while you're sipping cosmopolitans in Midtown, my father will be humiliating me in my own home."

"I thought you said Sarah invited you *there* for dinner."

"News flash. My father's obsessed with making some Italian soup he's discovered. He won't rest until everyone in the tri-state area has tasted some."

"You're having soup for dinner?"

I rolled over onto my back. Pieter meowed for me to throw him another Q-tip, but thinking about Friday's dinner made me far too depressed to engage in strenuous physical activity.

"It's *special* soup," I said sarcastically.

Downstairs I could hear the opening bars of yet another opera. Suddenly my father's voice boomed. *"Let all the cats out, or we'll have some mice to deal with."*

"Believe me," I said, "at this moment soup is the least of my problems."

That night when we sat down to eat, I tried to bring up the subject of Friday night's dinner as gently as possible.

"So, you're cooking dinner for Josh and his cousin on Friday," I said.

My dad had taken off his apron and the chef's hat. I looked at him critically. He couldn't help being mostly bald, but there was no excuse for the love handles he was developing. Could he possibly work them off in forty-eight hours? I wondered.

"Daniel, I'm happy to cook if you'd rather not," offered my mom.

"NO!" I shouted. She looked hurt.

"I'm not such a terrible cook," she said. It was a complete lie. My mother is the worst cook in the world.

"You know, Stalin probably didn't think he was such a terrible person," I pointed out.

"Jan, that is an *awful* thing to say," said my mother.

"Apologize to your mother," said my father.

Clearly this conversation had gotten off on the wrong foot. I decided it was time to take the high road.

"I'm sorry, Mom," I said. "I should not have compared your cooking to Stalin's extermination of the kulaks." I was glad to see the research I'd done for my essay on Stalin's purges was paying off. My mother didn't say she accepted my apology, which I thought was fairly rude, but I continued. "I just meant, maybe Dad should cook."

"Of course I'll cook," said my dad. He held up a wooden spoon and started conducting along with the CD. "*I will cook the meal for all the people. It will be so good that they will weeple*," he sang.

Was it really that impossible for my family to be normal for five minutes?

"The thing is . . ." I started. I needed to proceed delicately. "Maybe you could not sing along and, you know, not wear your chef's hat and the plastic apron." My dad looked at me. He still had his wooden spoon up in the air. "I mean, they're coming to meet you because you're a professor at an Ivy League school, so maybe you could try to look a little more . . . Ivy League."

My dad lowered the spoon and looked at me with a hurt expression. "You no like-a de apron?" he asked in a fake Italian accent.

"Not so much," I said.

"You no like-a de hat?"

"I believe my position on the hat has been firmly established."

"You no like-a de lyrics?"

"Maybe just not for Friday night. Then you could, you know, go back to your usual . . . thing."

My dad shrugged. "You no like, I no do," he said.

He and my mom looked at each other in their she'll-grow-out-of-it-someday way. Normally I might have taken this as an opportunity to point out that I was not the one whose idea of mature behavior involved leaping around the kitchen like a tone-deaf Pavarotti, but after the Stalin comment I decided not to press my luck.

"So, how are you doing with the applications?" my dad asked after we'd been sitting in silence for a few minutes.

"Fine," I said, spearing a pea with one tine of my fork.

They waited for me to elaborate. When I didn't, my mom asked, "Fine I don't want to talk about it, or fine they're getting done?"

"Just fine." I stabbed another pea and then a third. Lined up like that they looked pretty, like beads on a necklace.

Nobody said anything. I could practically hear my parents looking at each other.

"Jan, we don't want to meddle," my dad started.

"I think we meddle a lot less than other parents," my mom added.

"Parents always think they're less meddlesome and more permissive than other parents," I said.

"Be that as it may," my mom said, "we've been pretty good about letting you handle this whole application process on your own."

"You mean except for the part where you made me visit every single small liberal arts college in the Northeast, forbade my applying anyplace west of the Mississippi, and spent ten thousand hours *casually* mentioning how much you think I'd enjoy Amherst?" I picked up a strand of spaghetti with my fingers and dropped it into my mouth. Normally this is the kind of behavior that annoys my parents, but tonight they were too focused on getting information out of me to be distracted by the old bad-table-manners trick.

"Jan, you make it sound like we're tyrants," my dad said.

"Notice that *I* merely say what you've done and *you* conclude you're being tyrannical," I pointed out. In debate we learned the best way to win an argument is to let the other side get tied up by its own logic; in the case of my parents, it was almost too easy.

"The point your mother and I are trying to make . . ." my dad started to say.

I picked up my plate. It was time to bring out the heavy artillery.

"You know, I wish I could talk about this more," I said. "But I have a really big test tomorrow, and I'd better get cracking."

The day parents stop falling for the whole gotta-study-for-my-big-test-tomorrow routine is going to be an ugly one for teenagers everywhere.

When I got upstairs and saw the pile of college applications that lay on my green rug, I was forced to admit to myself the process was going "fine" only in the sense that nothing had actually happened and, therefore, nothing had yet gone wrong. Sitting at my tiny metal desk, I vowed to use my new incentive (*the registration line, the shy smile, I had no idea you were a student here . . .*) to finish my Wesleyan application *tout de suite*.

"What unique qualities could you contribute to the Wesleyan community?"

Well, that should be easy enough. What unique qualities could I contribute to the Wesleyan community? I started typing.

I have many unique qualities that I could contribute to the Wesleyan community. For example, I . . .

Sadly, nothing was coming immediately to mind. Perhaps I needed to be a bit more savvy, approach the essay from an entirely different angle. A little self-deprecation would help the admissions committee see I was not one of those slightly-above-average applicants with an ego ten times the size of her GPA.

There are many unique qualities I could not *contribute to the Wesleyan community.*

Ha! That was certainly a *unique* opening.

For example, I do not speak a foreign language, and I have no athletic ability. I have never had the lead in a school play. I am incapable of mastering a musical instrument and can't dance. . . .

This was a little too easy. How profoundly depressing is it to realize at the advanced age of seventeen you actually have no unique qualities to contribute to anything?

I started again.

I am certainly a unique applicant who would contribute a great deal to the Wesleyan community. For example, I regularly spend hours in a special fantasy world that bears no relationship whatsoever to reality. . . .

"Jan, phone's for you." No doubt it was Rebecca, eager to share more details of her upcoming romantic evening with Brian. I could see it already: Rebecca accepted at Brown, jetting off to Paris for a weekend with her older lover. Me, rejected everywhere, sitting at home with my parents night after night listening as my father invented opera lyrics.

"Hello?"

"Jan?" An unfamiliar male voice.

"Yes?"

"It's Tom."

"Hi." *Why was this happening to me?* I dug my nails into my arm like I do at the dentist, hoping the pain would erase the memory of Tom trying to suck on my neck.

"You haven't been in history the last couple of days."

"Yeah, I know. I went to some college information sessions." Actually, I'd *meant* to go to the sessions, but then Rebecca and I just went to Starbucks instead. It was probably good that I was getting so familiar with the Starbucks menu since I'd need to get a job there after being rejected from every college I applied to.

"Oh. How were they?"

"Informational."

"Well, that's good." The nail-digging trick wasn't working as well as it does at Dr. Monroe's. When I let go of my arm there was a line of purple half-moons on the inside of my wrist, but the memory of Tom's saliva was still as powerful as ever.

Tom cleared his throat. "The thing is, I was wondering if, ah . . ."

I had a very bad feeling about where his sentence was heading. "Um, Tom, I have to go."

"What?"

"I have to go." I racked my brain for any legitimate-sounding reason I might have to suddenly get off the phone. "My, ah, parents don't like me talking on the phone on school nights."

He sounded as surprised to hear what I'd said as I was to have said it. "Wow. They're, like, really strict, aren't they?"

"You don't know the half of it." I shook my head to show how crazy they were, but then I remembered he couldn't see me. I tried a long-suffering sigh instead.

Tom was clearly unmoved by my Academy Award–winning depiction of a misunderstood teen.

"So, is it, like, a religious thing?"

"Um, not exactly." I don't know too much about Judaism, but I'm pretty sure it doesn't have a rule that forbids talking on the phone on school nights.

"Okay, I'd better talk fast, then. I was thinking that, you know, maybe you'd, like, want to go out sometime."

There was silence.

I knew Tom was waiting for me to respond, but all I could think to say was, *This is what you get for not saying no, this is what you get for not saying no, this is what you get for not saying no.* After the first couple of repetitions, the sentence began to have an almost hypnotic quality. I could feel myself being lulled into a trance.

Meanwhile, the silence grew.

"Jan?" Tom said finally. "You still there?"

"The thing is, Tom, I wish I could, but I can't."

"You can't?" He sounded annoyed and embarrassed, like someone had just told him his fly was undone.

"I just can't."

More silence.

Finally I couldn't take it anymore.

"It's not that I don't want to," I lied.

"Oh?" he said in his regular voice.

"It's just . . . my parents. . . ."

"Your . . . oh, right. Oh. Sure. Wow." He laughed.

"Yeah, I mean, if they won't let you talk on the phone, they're not gonna let you . . ."

"Right." We were both laughing now. I was so relieved that my laugh wasn't even fake.

"That's a bummer," Tom said. "You're so cool about it. Don't you get pissed off?"

"Yeah, well . . . what can I do? They're my parents." I sounded saintly as a March sister.

"Sure," said Tom, sounding bored. "Well, I guess you'd better get going, then."

"Yeah," I said.

"Well, bye." He hung up.

"Bye," I cooed.

I hung up the phone feeling the kind of happiness you only experience after dodging a bullet. I was so relieved I even made up a little dance and named it the "Tom Richmond Will Never Bother Me Again Jig."

Whoever said honesty is the best policy obviously didn't have much experience with dating.

CHAPTER ELEVEN

Rebecca and I had prepared for Josh and Sarah's coming over as if we were the FBI and dinner was the War on Terrorism. Sometimes it is an excellent thing to have an It Girl for a best friend because she knows a lot of things about entertaining that I would never have guessed. For example, the rules and regulations of hostessing:

1. **A good hostess always devotes herself to the least-popular guest.** (That meant, since Sarah would be talking to my mom about how much fun life had been back in the seventies, and Josh's cousin would be talking to my dad about Columbia, it was clearly *my* job to entertain Josh.)
2. **A good hostess never overdresses, yet always manages to look comfortable and sexy.** (That was why I was going to wear my see-through shirt with a lacy tank top under it.)
3. **A good hostess is relaxed; she does not spend the evening jumping up and down to bring things in from the kitchen and clear the table.** (That explained why it was my mom's job to serve and clean up.)

In addition to educating me about being a perfect

hostess, Rebecca lent me her new lipstick, lip liner, and eyelash curler. Even when she has a big date at The Madison, a friend knows when you need MAC help way more than she does.

The problem is, there's only so much the right outfit and makeup can do when you're in the world's least-seductive setting. I mean, the bar at The Madison Hotel is a classy Midtown institution. It's got modular furniture covered in crisp white cotton, and the only people there (besides underage drinkers like me and Rebecca) are models and power brokers, who sip ice-cold martinis as they discuss their latest transatlantic flights. Everyone's dressed in Armani, Prada, or Versace, and there's no sound but the tinkling of ice cubes in metal shakers and the subdued laughter and sotto-voce conversation of the rich and the beautiful.

In contrast, when you first walk into my house in Brooklyn, you are greeted by our one-hundred-and-twenty-pound Labrador retriever, who lunges at your chest barking hysterically until you bend down to scratch his stomach.

The furniture in my house isn't white—it's covered with pet hair.

There is no Armani, Prada, or Versace as far as the eye can see.

The only thing that tinkles here is Brueghel, who sometimes gets so excited about being scratched that he has an accident.

On Friday at T minus two hours and fifteen minutes, I finished my physics homework. At T minus one hour and fifteen minutes, as I was trying to drown my jealousy of Rebecca and my anxiety over what was about to take place in my living room in a *Seinfeld* rerun, my mother stomped downstairs like a pro wrestler. She was wearing the black turtleneck sweater I'd worn to Richie's party.

"Yahn, have you worn my sweater?"

"Um, I don't think so."

"You don't *think* so?"

I didn't say anything. I've found if you ignore them, sometimes parents will eventually disappear.

"Hello! Do not ignore me when I am speaking directly to you." She stepped between me and the TV.

And sometimes they won't.

"Let's just say it's not impossible," I offered.

She put her hands on her hips. "What's the rule on wearing my things?"

"Yahn can wear Mom's things, but only if she asks first." I said it like I was reciting something I'd memorized for school.

"So what's wrong with this picture?"

"Um, I take it the answer is not that you're standing between me and the television."

"Yahn—" My mom has this voice she gets that's kind of like Brueghel's growl when a strange dog wanders onto our Cape Cod property. If you had to translate it into words, it would probably come out as, "Don't make me kill you."

"Okay, okay," I said, standing up and throwing my hands in the air. "I wore your sweater without asking. I'm sorry. I'm sorry. I'm sorry. It won't happen again."

"That's all I wanted to hear," said my mom. She moved away from the television and started counting out napkins to set the table. "You can watch your show now."

But I had no more time for television.

The time had come to launch Operation Josh.

When the doorbell rang I was upstairs prepared to wait. I know it can be a bad idea to plan a dramatic entrance when you're as klutzy as I am, but Rebecca and I had decided it would be smart to make Josh suffer alone with the parents for a few minutes. (Actually, it was Rebecca's plan. I wanted to keep Josh and my mother and father as far away from each other as humanly possibly so he wouldn't start having doubts about the stability of my genetic makeup, but Rebecca insisted my parents probably couldn't do anything too humiliating in just a few minutes. She said the benefits of forcing Josh to suffer alone with the parents for a little while—which would make him incredibly grateful and relieved to see me when I finally did come downstairs—far outweighed the risk that after spending a few minutes with my mother and father, he would run screaming into the night.)

Rebecca said I should stay upstairs until there was a lull in the conversation and then go down. The problem was, I couldn't really hear whether people were talking. Not only was Brueghel still barking like crazy, my dad had put some music on and everyone seemed to have gone into the kitchen, which is at the opposite end of the house from my room. I was just getting ready to sneak to the top of the stairs and await a moment of awkward silence into which I would glide, effortlessly rescuing my guests, when my mom shouted up, "Yahn, come down, everyone's here."

Just one more thing that never happens at The Madison.

I made it down the stairs without tripping, which didn't actually matter since nobody could see me. Then I turned the corner to go into the kitchen. Rebecca wanted me to say something funny and flirtatious right off the bat, just to establish "energy" with Josh. I liked her idea, but so far nothing funny or flirtatious had presented itself to me. Plus, how flirtatious can you be with your parents standing a mere two feet away? Rebecca kept saying how attractive and *transgressive* it would be if I just flirted up a storm and acted like they weren't there, but I'd pretty much settled for just saying, "Hey," and trying not to slide down the stairs on my butt. It's always a good idea in these situations to keep your expectations on the low side.

And then I was in the kitchen and it was suddenly clear that no matter how low my expectations were, they weren't low enough.

"Where's Josh?" I hadn't meant to say it quite so loudly. My mom, dad, Sarah, and some guy I'd never seen before looked up at me.

"Hello there, Jan," said Sarah. "Josh isn't coming. He's at a soccer tournament. That's an absolutely *beautiful* shirt!" My dad took one look at my shirt and promptly looked away. He walked some plates of appetizers over to the coffee table while Sarah gave me a hug.

I felt numb all over, but not the way my leg had felt numb when Josh rested his foot on it. Imagine you had an operation where they were supposed to amputate your arm, only when you woke up the surgeon told you they'd amputated the wrong one by mistake.

That's the kind of numb I felt.

"Hello, Jan." Josh's cousin looked and dressed nothing like Josh. He was shorter than I was and had horrible greasy hair he kept touching. He was wearing a suit and *white* sneakers.

"Jan, this is Henry. Henry, this is Jan, Josh's friend." Henry came over to me and stuck out his hand. When I gave him mine, he shook it very formally. Up, down. His palm was sweaty, but I had to wait until he looked away to wipe it on my skirt.

I felt like I was underwater. My dad said something to Sarah, and Henry said something to my mom, and then we all moved into the living room. I sat at the end of the sofa looking at everyone and trying to figure out why the gods were so desperate to punish me. I think I'm a good person. I mean, maybe I don't spend all my free time fighting to end world poverty . . . but I recycle!

Can't the universe give me a break?

"Jan?" Suddenly everyone was looking at me. *Well, folks, check it out, because this is something you'll want to remember: how I looked right before I jumped off the Brooklyn Bridge.*

"Sorry?"

"I was just asking you if you were interested in Columbia as well." Henry's voice squeaked. He stopped touching his sticky hair long enough to pull at the knot of his tie.

"Oh, ah, no. Maybe Wesleyan."

"Josh likes Wesleyan, too," said Sarah.

"I didn't know Wesleyan was your first choice," said my parents in unison.

"I'm not saying it's my first choice," I said, trying not to snarl. "I just said I'm *interested* in it."

"Wesleyan has an excellent reputation," squeaked Henry. "But I think I'd find Middletown just a tad provincial." *Provincial: of the provinces; not sophisticated or fashionable.* Henry wasn't the only one who'd studied for his SATs.

I shrugged. In his white sneakers Henry didn't exactly strike me as the most sophisticated, fashionable person I'd ever met. Unless he meant he needed to find someplace that was sophisticated enough not to ostracize poorly dressed midgets with acne.

"Are you hoping to stay on the East Coast?" my mom asked Henry.

"I feel my personality is more suited to the East, yes." Was it my imagination or was Henry checking out the see-through of my see-through shirt? I folded my arms over my chest and glared at him.

Why was this happening to me? Right about now, Josh and I were supposed to be giving each other knowing looks, rolling our eyes about how boring this whole "family dinner thing" was turning out to be.

JOSH: *(Walking over and sitting on the floor next to Jan's chair.)* Are you as bored as I am?

JAN: *(Whispering.)* Oh, definitely. I don't know how I'm going to make it through this.

JOSH: *(Smiling up at her and taking her hand.)* Well, I know how I'm going to get through it.

JAN: *(Puzzled.)* Really? How's that?

JOSH: I'm going to think about being alone with you later. *(He smiles up at her and brushes a stray curl out of her eyes.)*

CURTAIN

". . . say that Harvard doesn't have its advantages." Henry looked over at me. "Wouldn't you agree?"

Like I cared about Harvard. Like I cared about *Henry*. Like I cared about anything.

"I wouldn't know," I said.

Clearly Henry was too *provincial* to understand something as subtle as sarcasm. "Well, I think I can safely say the statistics will bear me out. Not that theirs is the best business school anymore. I'd have to say it's a toss-up between Columbia and Wharton." He turned to my dad. "I'm planning to be an economics major."

My dad nodded. He was wearing a pair of gray pants and a blue button-down, and he looked surprisingly normal. Just my luck, the whole family was looking its best for Horrible Henry and his Harvard Hopes.

"Last time I talked to Josh, he said he and Leslie were both applying early to Brown," said Henry.

Whatever you do, do not ask who Leslie is. Do not ask who Leslie is. Do not ask who Leslie is.

I turned to Sarah. "Who's Leslie?" I hoped my tone didn't betray my growing inner hysteria. I sounded light. Casual. *What's in this delicious soup? Have you noticed the weather's been unseasonably warm lately? Is that a new haircut? Who's Leslie?*

"She's a friend of Josh's," said Sarah. "From Seattle."

Henry got a sly look on his face and raised his eyebrows at me, as if we were both in on some extraordinary secret. "Well, I guess you *could* call her a *friend*."

On the coffee table with the hors d'oeuvres were about half a dozen metal toothpicks for spearing the roasted peppers my dad had made. I was seriously considering taking one and stabbing Henry in the eye with it.

"Really?" asked Sarah. "I guess the mother's always the last to know."

"I guess," Henry said, still looking at me.

"But I'm pretty sure Josh isn't applying anywhere early," Sarah added. "I think I'd know *that*."

"Well," said my dad. "Why don't we start on the soup?" As my mom and Sarah started gathering up the plates from the coffee table and my dad headed into the kitchen, Henry followed me into the dining room.

"That's quite a shirt you have on there," he said. No wonder he'd been eyeing my chest—it was practically eye level for him.

"Mmmm," I said.

"Is that how all New York girls dress?"

"I wouldn't really know," I said.

"Because I can tell you right now, Columbia's *definitely* becoming my first choice." Henry gave a little cackle, pulled out a chair, and sat down.

No, not the eye. I've read the eye has surprisingly few nerve endings. It's the ear that's really painful. I'd go for the eardrum.

CHAPTER TWELVE

Not only did Brian and Rebecca stay out until two in the morning drinking cosmopolitans at The Madison, not only did they go back to his apartment and make out—without him either (a) drooling all over her or (b) asking her to just touch it once, he also invited her to a party Saturday night.

In other words, during the same twenty-four-hour period in which (a) my dreams of being with Josh were dashed by incontrovertible proof of his love for Brown-bound Leslie, and (b) I was eye raped by Henry the Horrible, my best friend was at a chic Midtown bar acquiring a cute, funny, sexually experienced boyfriend.

> *Of all the unique qualities I could contribute to the Wesleyan community, none seems so worth mentioning as the fact that I am a huge loser. Accepting Jan Miller guarantees no Wesleyan student need ever again feel inadequate. "At least I'm not Jan Miller" will become the rallying cry of the Wesleyan campus. Who knows what heights Wesleyan graduates will achieve, safe in the knowledge that no matter how far they fall, someone will always have fallen farther, fallen faster. . . .*

"I think you're overreacting." Rebecca and I were drinking cappuccinos at Bombshell, our favorite café in SoHo, where we'd planned to meet to celebrate our respective romantic victories. Needless to say, only one of us had anything to celebrate.

"Do you think Leslie has a tiny butt? I bet she has a tiny butt."

"Why are you worried about her butt? Sarah's, like, barely even heard of this girl. They probably went out for two seconds last spring, and Henry's just dumb enough to think they're still together."

I shook my head the whole time she was talking. "You don't understand. I had a *feeling* about Leslie. Just the way he said it." I made my voice airy and wistful. "Leslie." I turned to Rebecca. "See the difference?"

"Well, I see that you're *crazy*."

"Josh probably told Sarah he had a soccer tournament this weekend, and really he flew out to Seattle for a secret romantic rendezvous with blond-haired, blue-eyed Leslie and her teeny tiny butt."

"You're insane, do you know that? Sometimes I seriously worry that you have no grip on reality whatsoever."

"Do you realize Henry actually thought he had a *chance*? He *flirted* with me. When he left he gave me a really significant look like this." I lowered my chin and stared at Rebecca. "And then he said, 'I have the feeling this isn't the last time we'll cross paths.'" I shuddered. "Be honest. Do I give off a vibe that says, 'No, handsome stud, I don't want you to make a pass at me,' while at the same time communicating, 'Hello there, acne-ridden dwarf. Promise me we'll meet again.'"

"Tom Richmond is *not* an acne-ridden dwarf."

"*I almost drowned on his saliva,*" I nearly shouted. "What are you not understanding? *He endangered my life.*" A woman sitting nearby looked up from what she was reading and stared at us.

Rebecca lowered her voice almost to a whisper. "Here's the question you should be asking—why must you insist on pursuing high-school boys?"

"*I'm* not pursuing *them. They're* pursuing *me,*" I hissed.

"Come with me to this party tonight. We need to find you an older boyfriend." She mimed taking a drag of an imaginary cigarette and adopted a French accent. "You are *much* too sophisticated to party with zeez silly children, dahling."

Let's see: cool party full of older guys with Rebecca Larkin; It Girl. Or night at home with Mom and Dad Miller; Losers. As you can imagine, I agonized over my options.

Brian's friend's apartment was in a fancy building on Central Park West. While we rode up in the elevator with the elevator man (not to be confused with the doorman), I started to get nervous that everyone was going to be really old and wearing suits and stuff, but the host (or the person I assumed was the host, since he opened the door for us) was wearing a blue button-down and a pair of khakis, and he looked like he was probably in his early twenties. He was also extremely cute, and I was glad I'd let Rebecca convince me to take the see-through top out

122

for another spin. Maybe Rebecca was right. Maybe my whole problem *did* stem from being too sophisticated for high-school boys.

The guy, whose name was Joel, led us down a long hall, past the kitchen and into the living room, where he called, "Hey, Brian," and a cute guy with dark hair, who was *also* wearing a pair of khakis and a blue button-down shirt, came over. As I looked around, I realized almost every guy in the room was wearing some variation on the blue-shirt-and-khakis outfit. The women were mostly wearing black pants and different-colored tops. The apartment looked exactly like a spread in the Pottery Barn catalog.

"Hi," said Brian. He looked Rebecca up and down and whistled softly at her backless dress. "You look great." He kissed her on the cheek.

"This is Jan," she said. He shook my hand.

"Nice to meet you," he said. "I'll introduce you around."

After being introduced to four or five identical-looking people, I stopped even trying to remember who was who. As far as I could tell, all the guys looked just like Joel and all the girls looked just like Joel's girlfriend, Diana. There were about fifteen Dianas and twenty or so Joels, though I might have been counting some people twice and missing others. The only person who didn't blend into the crowd was a guy named Ken, who, in addition to obviously being gay, was wearing jeans and a black turtleneck sweater. He was very handsome, and he kept looking around the party like he couldn't believe how boring it was. He was talking to a woman whose long, curly hair made her slightly different from all the other straight-hair Dianas.

Brian was nice about trying to stay close to Rebecca and me, and he was working hard not to make me feel like a third wheel. Unfortunately that meant he kept asking me questions about myself, each of which threw me into a panic since I don't know nearly as much about NYU as Rebecca does.

"We had one of your film professors visiting my freshman year. I didn't take a class with him, but I heard he was great. I think his name was Moser or Muller? I can't remember. Did you ever take a class with him?"

I had an olive pit in my mouth and wasn't sure what to do with it. "Um, no, I haven't, ah, taken any film. Where did you go to college?"

"I went to Brown."

"Oh, really? That's where Rebecca—" Miraculously I stopped myself from finishing my sentence. *Oh, really? That's where Rebecca applied early.* Rebecca and Brian were both looking at me, but his was a look of curiosity and hers was one of horror. "Um, that's where Rebecca wanted to go."

"Really?" asked Brian. "You didn't tell me that."

"Well, you know," said Rebecca, glaring at me. "Sour grapes."

"Don't take it too hard," said Brian. "I'm sure you'll manage to cobble together a life that isn't *too* horrible."

"Thanks," said Rebecca. "I'll try to hold on to that."

He took our glasses. "I'll get you guys some more wine."

More people kept arriving, but it was hard to tell the new ones from the old ones since everyone looked the same. All the wine I had drunk wasn't helping, either. A few times I thought about trying to get involved in a conversation, but each group Brian introduced us to seemed to be arguing over something I knew nothing about. At one point, when Rebecca went to the bathroom, I drifted by three people who were talking loudly and gesturing a lot. As soon as I got near them, one of the guys turned to me and said, "Quick: Who do you think more people have heard of, Henry Kissinger or Madonna?"

"Ah, Madonna?" I answered.

He turned back to the other two, who'd also been waiting for my answer. They groaned as soon as I said, "Madonna," but he laughed triumphantly. "Told you!" he said to them. Then he turned back toward me. "Thanks," he said.

"No problem," I said. He was kind of cute. I tried to think of something flirtatious to say. "So who's this Henry Kissinger guy?"

He looked confused. "Wait, are you serious?"

I shook my head no, and he went back to talking to his friends.

Why is it that I attract people I want to repel and repel people I want to attract?

My search for the answer to this troubling question led me to the bar, which may have been why I started to get pretty drunk. At high-school parties it's understood that your goal is to chug down as much as possible as quickly as possible (since everyone else is trying to do the exact same thing). I was on my third glass of wine when I realized all the other guests were sipping their drinks without the same sense of panic that was driving me.

"If you keep drinking wine like that I'm checking you into the Betty Ford clinic," Rebecca said after I'd come back with my fourth full glass.

"What's that?"

"It's where the stars go to rehab."

I nodded. Surrounded by stars—that didn't sound so bad.

I was feeling a little dizzy, so I handed Rebecca my empty wineglass.

"What's more likely to blow our cover?" I asked her. "Throwing up, or a pithy anecdote about the college application process?"

"I think you'd better get a glass of water," she said. I was starting to get the feeling she regretted bringing me.

I went into the kitchen, where Ken was talking to one of the Joels.

"Well, hello there," he said. "Emerging from the lion's den, I see?"

"Ken, right?" The refrigerator was the kind with water and ice on the door, and I filled a glass and drank it.

"Good for you. Nice memory."

"Not really," I said. "You're the only one who's not wearing khakis."

He laughed. "Yes, it's a *tad* 'Still Life with Dockers' out there."

His friend laughed, too, but then he said, "Hey, wait a second!" and pointed at his khakis. He wasn't very tall, but there was definitely something cute about him.

Ken looked at me carefully. "It's none of my business, but isn't your friend a little young to be playing with grown-ups?"

Focus, Jan. Focus. "She's twenty-one," I said, trying to remember if that was the age we'd agreed to say we were.

"Darling," said Ken, "if she's twenty-one, I'm Donatella Versace."

"Well, Donatella, what makes you so sure she's underage?" I aimed to convey amusement rather than panic.

"A woman knows," he said, and he and his friend both laughed.

"Okay," I said, thinking, *Whatever.*

"Don't worry," he said, smiling at his friend. "I'll never tell."

"How old are *you*?" his friend asked me.

"How old are *you*?" I countered smoothly.

"She's feisty," the guy said to Ken. Then to me he said, "You're cute."

"Thanks," I said. The four glasses of wine I'd chugged may have been responsible for what I said next. "You're cute, too."

"I'll leave you two to chat," said Ken. He winked at me and then he left.

"So," said the guy.

"So," I said.

"I'm Alex," he said. He had reddish hair and tiny glasses. I don't normally go for redheads, but he had nice blue eyes.

"I'm Jan," I said.

"Are you twenty-one, too?" he asked.

I shrugged, hoping to convey I was an international woman of mystery rather than a drunken teenager. Alex walked over to me, and I could tell from how he held himself that he was even drunker than I was. He stopped about three inches away from my face.

"What year were you born?" he asked. I could smell alcohol on his breath and see the slight stubble of his beard. Not counting my dad, I'd never stood this close to someone who needed a shave.

"What are you, the bouncer?" I asked. My heart was pounding.

He didn't seem to be listening. "You are *extremely* cute, you know that?" he said. "*Extremely* cute." He leaned toward me and whispered in my ear. "You're cute enough to eat," he said. "I'd like to take you home with me and gobble you up."

How are you supposed to respond when a perfectly normal-looking guy suddenly starts talking like Hannibal Lecter?

"Um, thanks," I said.

He rubbed his cheek against mine. Stubble may look sexy, but it feels terrible.

"What do you say, little girl? Do you want to be

gobbled up?" He was slurring his words a little and leaning against me. "I could gobble you right up."

"Well, I'll definitely be sure to keep that in mind," I said, taking a step back. He swayed for a minute before catching himself on the counter. "It was nice meeting you, Alex."

"And you," said Alex.

I found Rebecca talking to one of the Joels. She was laughing at something he'd said, and she started to tell me about it, but I pulled her away and told her about what had happened with Alex. She didn't seem that impressed.

"I'm telling you," I said. "I felt like Clarice Starling."

"Weird," she said, shrugging.

"I can't believe that's what high-school guys turn into!"

"Jan, you can't judge grown men after dealing with just one of them." I wanted to point out that was exactly what she was doing with Brian, but instead I told her about Ken's guessing she wasn't really twenty-one. To my surprise, she didn't seem to care that much.

"Look, it's not like I'm *illegal*," she said. "I'm eighteen. In some countries I'd be too old to get married. I'd be an old maid." I had the feeling I wasn't the only one who was a little drunk.

"Yes, but we don't live in those countries," I pointed out. "Those countries have camels and . . . you know, weird stringed instruments. It's completely different."

"This is true," she acknowledged. She looked over by the food, where Brian was talking to a man and a woman who had their arms around each other. "How cute is he?" she asked.

Brian looked up and saw her looking at him. He smiled. He had broad shoulders and ruddy cheeks. "He *is* cute," I agreed. He said something to the couple he was talking to and walked over to us.

"Is there anyone here you'd like me to introduce you to?" he asked me.

"Me? Oh, ah, no. That's okay." The last thing I needed was another cannibalistic come-on.

He looked around the room. "Yeah, it's a pretty lame lot. Sorry about that."

"No, it's not that. I just—"

"She's very particular," said Rebecca. "She won't settle for just anyone."

"Unlike you," said Brian. Rebecca smiled up at him, and then they kissed.

Could this night get any more depressing?

"So," said Brian, turning to me. "What are you looking for in a man?"

I looked around the khaki-filled room. "How about jeans?"

By midnight all my energy was going into trying not to puke, avoiding another conversation with Alex, and figuring out how to get home since "Don't forget about my curfew" seemed like the kind of thing Rebecca wouldn't want me to say in front of Brian. Meanwhile, I couldn't help noticing that in addition to having the same pants and shirts, all the Joels seemed to be wearing identical shoes and watches. It was like a scene from *Attack of the Clones*.

Just as I decided it was time to take a cab home alone,

embracing freedom over solvency, Rebecca came up to me.

"Brian wants to get out of here. Do you feel like going?" Actually, the only thing I felt like doing was puking, but I didn't want to mention that. We got our coats and said good-bye to the original Joel. I was afraid we'd run into Alex as we were leaving, but he seemed to have disappeared.

Outside, Brian hailed a cab and the three of us got in. "We're making three stops," he told the driver. "First is Seventy-seventh and Amsterdam and the second is—"

"Actually, we're making two stops," said Rebecca. She was smiling.

"Three," said Brian, but he was smiling also.

"Two."

"Three."

"You folks need to make up your mind," said the driver. I couldn't have agreed with him more.

"Come on," said Brian.

"No, you come on," said Rebecca.

Will you both come on! I felt like shouting.

"You know you're irresistible," said Brian quietly.

"So why are you resisting me?" Rebecca asked.

Brian groaned. "Okay, sir, better give the lady what she wants. Two stops. The first is Seventy-seventh and Amsterdam and the second is—" He turned to me. "Downtown, right?"

"No, Brooklyn. Park Slope," I said, before I remembered I was supposed to live by NYU. When I was younger, I went through a phase where I read a lot of espionage novels, and for a while I'd been really into the idea of being a spy. But if my behavior tonight was any indication, it was clear that I was not cut out for intelligence work.

I gave the driver my address.

"I didn't realize you lived in Brooklyn," he said. "How's that commute?"

"Oh, ah, not too bad. It's, ah, it's okay."

"Good," he said, nodding. Clearly I wasn't the only one who shouldn't try for a career as a covert operative. Brian must have been the most naive person on the planet.

By the time they got out of the cab, I was so tired I didn't think I could stay awake until I got home. Maybe Rebecca was right—maybe high-school guys *are* lame.

But if you want my opinion, the alternative is even lamer.

CHAPTER
THIRTEEN

I couldn't reach Rebecca on her cell Sunday, which meant there was nothing for me to do all day except contemplate the train wreck that was my life. Sitting at the computer trying yet again to come up with reasons I was a unique candidate for admission to Wesleyan, I started making a list of everything that was good about my life and everything that was bad. The results weren't pretty.

GOOD	BAD
Don't have cancer	Have fat butt
Not starving/homeless	Will never be accepted to college
Not pregnant teen	Will probably die a virgin

I kept moving "Parents not dead" and "Best friend is very cool It Girl" from one column to the other.

Rogier was supposed to be home at five, since Yale gets a whole week off for Thanksgiving, but he called at three to say he was thinking about staying in New Haven and coming down to New York on Monday instead. You know things are bad when you can't even be pleased your mother and your perfect brother are having a huge fight. I was half listening to her tell him how inconsiderate he is and half thinking about how I'd look in a McDonald's uniform when all of a sudden my mom shouted, "Oh, that's wonderful, Rogier. So you can be exhausted and wind up having a car accident."

What would my life be like if Rogier died?

Would Josh come to the funeral?

Setting: *A funeral home in Park Slope.*

Scene: *A crowd of mourners slowly files past Jan, murmuring their condolences. Josh waits patiently in one of the pews. As the last person exits, Josh makes his way over to where Jan, model thin from grief, stands alone.*

JAN: *(Holding her hands out to him.)* It was good of you to come.

JOSH: *(Taking her hands and squeezing them.)* I am so sorry for your loss. *(Jan nods but says nothing. The grief that has made it impossible for her to eat for the past few weeks has also caused her hair to become straight, and Josh brushes a strand out of her eyes. There is a long pause.)* The thing is . . . I know this isn't the time or the place for confessions, but . . .

JAN: *(Smiling.)* Josh, I always thought we could be honest with each other. If something's on your mind, I want you to tell me.

JOSH: Well, Jan, I . . . *(He abruptly takes Jan in his arms.)* I love you, Jan. I hate myself for saying it here at your brother's funeral, but I never realized

how much I loved you until now, and I can't keep
silent another minute. *(He pulls her toward him.)*
Tell me you feel the same way I do. Tell me you
love me.
JAN: Oh, Josh, I— *(He presses his lips down on hers.)*

CURTAIN

Of course Rogier's death didn't do anything about the
Leslie factor. She was the one who needed to die. Only
did I really want Josh grieving over his dead girlfriend?

JOSH: *(Taking Jan in his arms.)* I love you, Jan.
JAN: I love you too, Josh. *(They embrace.)*
JOSH: *(Breaking away from her.)* I can't. It's too soon. I
still love . . . Leslie.

CURTAIN

No, that wouldn't do at all. What I needed wasn't
for Leslie to die, what I needed was for her to get really
really fat.

JOSH: *(Looking shocked.)* Leslie! Is that you?
LESLIE: *(Unwrapping a Snickers bar.)* It's me, Josh. It's
your darling Leslie. Only I'm a size twenty-eight
now.

CURTAIN

I felt better already.

* * *

The comfort provided by the image of Josh trying to get his arms around a suddenly obese Leslie lasted right up until Monday morning, when Rebecca informed me that Saturday night she had slept at Brian's apartment.

"You stayed *over*?" Students were no longer confined to school, and Rebecca and I were celebrating the administration's newfound confidence in us by cutting math. "What about your parents?"

"They were in D.C. at a fund-raiser."

"Wow," was all I could think of to say.

Rebecca nodded and took a sip of her cappuccino. Then she gave me a significant look.

"What?"

"What, what?" she asked, abruptly picking up her bag and digging through it.

"What's that look?"

"What look?" She practically had her entire head inside her bag.

I waited until she finally emerged and gave her the look back. "*That* look." Suddenly I had a horrifying thought. "Did you have sex with him?"

So this was my destiny—Jan Miller: Last American Virgin.

"Not exactly."

Now I was getting really annoyed. "Not *exactly*?"

"Well, we didn't have sex-sex. But we, you know . . ." Rebecca wasn't giving me the look anymore. In fact, she wasn't looking at me at all.

"What do you mean 'you know'?" I laughed. "What, did you touch it once?"

Rebecca didn't laugh, and she didn't look at me. She was staring into her cappuccino like she had never seen anything in her life as fascinating as foamed milk.

"Um, *hello*!" I said. "Are you not going to elaborate on this at all?"

She shrugged. "The thing is, Jan, it's kind of private." She looked up at me. "It's between me and Brian."

Was this actually happening? "What are you *talking* about? How can you have privacy with a guy who thinks you're in college?" I started laughing again, but Rebecca didn't join me.

She looked back at her coffee. "You're just jealous." Her tone was downright icy.

"I'm jealous? I'm *jealous*? I'm jealous you're in a 'relationship' with someone who thinks you're twenty-one?" Now I wasn't laughing either.

"Sometimes you can be *such* a bitch, Jan, do you know that?" She stood up and put on her coat. "Maybe if you tried having a *real* relationship instead of an *imaginary* one, you'd know what I'm talking about."

And with that she stormed out of Starbucks.

I couldn't believe it. How could *Rebecca* be mad at *me* when all I'd done was point out the truth. How was *I* the one in an imaginary relationship when *she* was the one with the boyfriend she couldn't take to the prom because he thought her prom had been *four years ago*? I was a bitch? *I* didn't understand a real relationship?

I had cut math for *this*?

* * *

I couldn't really see any reason to hang out at Starbucks all by myself, so I just went to English and sat at my desk waiting for the bell to ring. Josh showed up a few minutes later and came right over to where I was sitting. I was still so pissed, I barely noticed.

"Hey," he said. He was wearing a Michigan T-shirt.

Was I going to have to apply to Michigan now?

"Hey," I said. It was hard to know who I was angrier at: Josh for bailing on dinner or Rebecca for bailing on me. In any event, I didn't feel the rush I usually experience when I'm within five feet of him. (Though I may have felt a tiny shiver of it when Mandy Johnson walked in and looked over at us like she was having her own fantasies of a funeral—mine.)

"I heard dinner was fun," he said. "Henry thought your parents were really cool."

I shrugged. "They're not," I said, glancing up at him.

He barely cracked a smile. "He thought *you* were cool, too."

Compared to Henry, I *am* cool. "Oh," I said. I took out my notebook.

"Listen, um." Josh was acting really strange. He stood right next to my desk, looking around the room like he'd lost something. Then he looked at me for a split second and looked away as soon as we made eye contact. Finally, he put his backpack down and slid into the seat next to mine. "Henry thought you were *really* cool."

"So?" I couldn't stop thinking about what Rebecca had said. What *exactly* were she and Brian doing that was

138

so incredibly private she couldn't even tell her so-called best friend about it?

"So . . ." Josh turned his palms up and raised his shoulders a little, like that one word contained a really significant question I was supposed to answer. He was still avoiding looking in my direction, and if I hadn't been so mad I might have been pleased that now *he* was the one who seemed nervous around *me*.

"Look, Josh, what are you getting at?" Rebecca and I had been best friends since second grade. We told each other *everything*. I mean, as far as I was concerned practically the whole *point* of fooling around with a guy was to tell Rebecca about it. Now, suddenly, she had this whole *private* life she couldn't share with me because it was too *special*.

Josh finally looked at me, but I kept staring at him without saying anything until he broke down and looked away. "Henry wanted to know if he could . . . you know . . . I mean . . . if you would . . . you know, maybe . . ." His cheeks were getting red. He bounced his feet up and down nervously.

If you asked me, *Rebecca* was the one who was being a bitch. Where did she get off saying that unless you were touching Mr. Second-Year Law Student "just once" you weren't *mature* enough to understand sex?

I was imagining saying these things to Rebecca's face, when all of a sudden I registered what it was Josh was struggling to articulate. I snapped instantly back into focus. "Henry wants to go *out* with me? He told you to ask me to go out with him?" I had officially entered the twilight zone.

Josh was looking more and more uncomfortable. "I know your, ah, love life isn't exactly any of my business."

"You're right, Josh, it's none of your business."

He started cracking his knuckles. "The thing is, he asked me to see what the deal was."

"Well, I'll tell you what the deal is. The deal is: no deal." We were staring into each other's eyes, but the look I was giving him wasn't flirtatious. It was murderous.

"Okay, that's cool." He'd stopped bouncing his legs and his face was beginning to approach its normal color.

"Thanks, Josh. I really appreciate how *cool* you and Henry seem to think I am." I opened my notebook and turned to face the front of the room like I was just dying for Mr. Kryle to arrive so class could start.

"Hey, easy there. You don't have to get all bitchy about it." Josh gave a little laugh, but I didn't see what was so funny about two people calling me a bitch in the space of a few hours.

"Oh, I'm sorry, Josh," I said sarcastically. "Am I not being *cool* enough for you?"

He had put one of his hands on my desk when I first said "No deal" to going out with Henry, but now he snatched it away. We stared at each other angrily for a minute before he stood up, grabbing his bag.

"Whatever," he said.

And then he walked to the other side of the room and sat down next to Mandy Johnson.

CHAPTER FOURTEEN

June 15

Dear Diary,

I can't believe today is the last day of eighth grade!!!! I'm soooo psyched for high school!!!! Rebecca and I went by Banana Republic at lunch, and they had this awesome sweater on sale. I bought it for the first day of ninth grade, and Rebecca said it's definitely a sign of how high school is going to be lucky for me (and for her, too, natch).

Rebecca says we're going to totally ignore the freshman boys right off and see if there are cute sophomores. High-school parties are going to be awesome, b/c high-school guys are extremely cool. Rebecca and I agreed that we should have sophomore boyfriends when we're freshmen, junior boyfriends when we're sophomores, and senior boyfriends when we're juniors. Then when we're seniors, we'll either have boyfriends who are in college or take a year just to be single and hang out together before we graduate. Also, we're going to go to Europe for the summer between high

school and college, and we don't want to be tied
down since we'll probably have European
boyfriends while we're over there.
　　The world is our oyster! TTFN!

The last thing I had planned on doing when I got home was making myself feel even worse than I already did by taking a trip down memory lane. But the Williams essay asked applicants to "Contrast the *you* graduating from high school with the *you* entering high school," and I couldn't think of a single thing about me that had changed since junior high except I'd finally stopped trying to blow-dry my hair straight.

I ended up in the basement, where there are tons of boxes with all our old papers and clothes and stuff. I found the box with my eighth-grade work, and it was kind of embarrassing. I did a big paper that year titled "Anorexia: The Silent Killer," and reading it made me wonder if my career goals had once included a desire to be a staff writer for *The National Enquirer*. The introduction ends, "These girls are dying of hunger but refuse to eat. They are screaming for help, but no one can hear them. An epidemic. A tragedy. Anorexia: The Silent Killer."

I made a mental note not to leave for college without first burning everything I'd written during the twentieth century.

For some reason the diary was at the bottom of the box marked JAN'S SCHOOLWORK: 7TH AND 8TH GRADE. As soon as I saw it, I remembered all the other diaries just like it I'd had back when I was a kid. I was always buying these pretty clothbound books at stores that sell things like scented candles and tiny pillows embroidered with corny sayings and then forgetting about them. On the first page of a new book I'd write THIS DIARY BELONGS TO JAN MILLER!!! DO NOT TOUCH!!! IF LOST PLEASE RETURN TO JAN MILLER. Then I'd write down my phone number and address, including *USA* (like I ever left the continental United States). But I rarely actually *wrote* in the diary. There'd be a long entry from the day I bought it, then another one the next day, and within a week I'd stop writing altogether. I don't remember what inspired the entry from the last day of eighth grade, but I do remember the sweater. It was a soft, gray cardigan I brought up to Cape Cod and immediately lost.

The Fantasy of High School: Parties with sophisticated older guys. Traveling through Europe with Rebecca.

The Reality of High School: Me. Alone. Rummaging around in the basement.

"Mom, are you downstairs?" It was Rogier.

His feet and shins appeared at the top of the stairs. "Mom?"

"Nope, it's Jan. When did you get home?"

"Oh, hey." He came down and sat on the bottom step, waving a CD in my direction. "I just got back a few hours ago. I went out to get this."

Every time Rogier comes home from Yale he has a new haircut. Over the summer it was kind of shaggy, but now it was short and preppy looking. Rebecca thinks it's because each of his girlfriends encourages him to cut it how she likes it. According to her theory, this new look meant Larissa was out of the picture.

"Do you know where Mom and Dad are?"

I shook my head.

"'Cause I think they want us all to go out for dinner or something, but I was going to meet Larissa later, and I need to know the plan."

Apparently Rebecca's haircut theory was incorrect. "Mom and Dad will freak if you go out tonight."

Rogier shrugged, but he looked a little nervous. "So," he said, leaning against the wall. "How's it going?"

"Okay, I guess," I said. When I was younger I wanted that older brother who is incredibly wise and gives his younger sister tons of advice and has all these really hot friends who tease her in this brotherly way except for the one who falls madly in love with her. Then he and the girl's brother have this big fight one night out in the rain because the brother's all, like, "You're not going out with my sister!" and the friend's, like, "I love her, man."

Then they make up and everyone goes to the prom.

Unfortunately, Rogier never really had that many friends, and the few he did have were such incredible dorks that if one of them had asked me out, I would have had to kill myself immediately. Also, I can't exactly imagine Rogier getting all worked up about my honor like the brothers in movies and on TV. If I told him about that guy Alex, at the party, he'd probably just say, "Weird," or something like that. He definitely wouldn't go off and challenge him to a duel or anything.

"Rogier?" He was staring off into space.

"Yeah?"

"Is college different from high school?"

"Sure," he said, pushing off the wall. He started to go upstairs.

"No, I mean *really* different. Like, completely different."

"What do you mean?" He turned to me.

"Well, I mean, is it like the difference between junior high and high school or is it the difference between Earth and Mars?"

"I've never been to Mars," he said.

"Ha ha." Sometimes Rogier can be as annoying as my parents.

"I don't know, Jan. Yeah, it's different. I mean, you don't have Mom and Dad breathing down your neck all the time."

Considering my parents were the least of my worries at the moment, that wasn't too comforting.

"What about socially? Like, guy–girl stuff."

Rogier shrugged. "I didn't really have much 'guy–girl' stuff at Lawrence."

"Could you use your imagination for, like, a *second*?"

"Jan, I don't know. Yes, it's different." He started walking upstairs.

"Fine," I said.

"I mean, I think it is," he added, turning around. He stopped and thought about it. "I don't know," he said finally. "Maybe it's not that different."

"Great," I said.

It was not what I had wanted to hear.

Maybe Rebecca and I would have made up if it was a regular week, but because of Thanksgiving, Rebecca left for Puerto Rico with her family Monday night. I kind of hoped she might call me from there (Rebecca's parents, unlike mine, do not see long-distance phone calls as a costly invention the telecommunications industry recently thought up to hoodwink us), but she didn't.

I ended up spending almost the whole vacation crossing things off my long-term to-do list; by Saturday night I'd cleaned out my closet, given myself a manicure and pedicure, put all my old letters into chronological order, and started the research for a history term paper due in January. Any minute now, I'd be ready to start on those college essays.

Maybe I was bored, lonely, and pathetic, but at least I wasn't disorganized.

There was a knock at my door.

"Yeah?"

Rogier poked his head in. "Do you want to go shoot some pool?"

"Okay," I said. I was surprised Rogier wanted to play pool with me since he's really great at pool and I really just suck. It's tragic because I'm desperate to be a good pool player. Having worked my way backward through the Julia Roberts canon, I've determined that my personal pool-playing goal is embodied by a scene in *Mystic*

Pizza—one of her earliest movies—where the rich college kids are feeling superior to the poor townies, and then Julia, who's a townie, embarrasses them by kicking their asses at pool. Her triumph is compounded, obviously, by the fact that she has on a tiny little black skirt, and all of them want to have sex with her.

I guess you could say the major difference between me and Julia, aside from how bad I am at pool, is that if I were a townie in a tiny black skirt, the rich college kids would be too busy making fun of how tight my skirt was to notice how badly I was playing.

"How come you're home on a Saturday night?" Rogier asked as we were walking down Seventh Avenue.

"How come *you're* home on a Saturday night?" I countered.

"Well, I don't really live here anymore, so I'm not technically home," he pointed out.

"Oh," I said. "I guess that makes me the official loser in the family."

"If you say so," he said.

"Rebecca and I had a fight," I said after we'd gone another block. "Plus, she goes to Puerto Rico with her family for Thanksgiving every year."

"So you'd be home even if you hadn't had a fight with Rebecca?"

"I guess so." While we walked, Rogier was flipping a quarter up in the air and then catching it, demonstrating the difference between his hand–eye coordination and mine. I can barely catch something if you hand it to me.

"Don't you have any friends besides Rebecca? Didn't you used to hang out with that girl . . . what was her name? Gabby? The one who was really cute?"

"You thought Gabby was cute?" I was so surprised I stopped walking. Rogier caught his quarter and turned to face me.

"I mean, I wasn't in love with her or anything, but yeah, I thought she was cute."

"I thought you didn't notice girls in high school."

Now it was Rogier's turn to be shocked. "Are you serious?"

"Well, why didn't you ask her out?"

We started walking again. "Um, in case you didn't notice, back then I wasn't exactly the most confident guy when it came to girls."

"Did you get . . . you know, are you more confident now?"

"Yeah, I'm more confident now," he said. Then he laughed. "When you start at zero, it's hard not to go up."

I didn't know what to make of that. I mean, clearly I wasn't exactly at zero since I wouldn't go out with a guy like Henry or someone who was a terrible kisser, like Tom. Did this mean my confidence could go *down* in college? That would certainly be a horrifying turn of events.

"So what happened to Gabby?" Rogier asked again.

"Why, do you want to ask her out?"

"Oh, yeah. I was hoping I could be one of the few guests at the Lawrence Academy prom who's older than the chaperones."

"You think older guys don't go out with high-school girls?" I thought about telling him how old Brian was, but I couldn't be one hundred percent sure he wouldn't tell my parents. And my parents telling her parents that she had a twenty-two-year-old boyfriend who thought she was in college probably wasn't going to do anything to improve things between Rebecca and me.

"I am fully aware that older guys go out with high-school girls," Rogier said. "I just don't happen to be a scumbag, okay? What is *with* you? All I asked is what happened to your friend Gabby."

I shrugged. "I don't know. She got kind of irritating."

"Fine," said Rogier. We kept walking in silence.

The thing is, by last spring Rebecca and I had decided *everyone* was kind of irritating except the two of us. Only that meant now that Rebecca and I were irritated with each other, there was no one left to hang out with.

After we'd played a couple of games, it occurred to me that I should take advantage of this golden opportunity to get a guy's perspective on the Josh situation. Unfortunately for me, it turned out Rogier had even less insight into the workings of the male mind than I.

"Why don't you just tell him you like him?" Rogier was racking up for yet another game in which he would mercilessly defeat me.

"You're not serious."

He placed the cue ball to the left of center and broke. Three balls went into various pockets. Needless to say, when I break, no balls go in.

"Stripes," he said. He looked at the table, deciding which shot to make next.

I tried a different approach. "I mean, what subtle stuff would you notice? Like, how guys don't like when girls don't eat, that kind of thing."

"What are you talking about?" Rogier, shockingly, missed his shot and stepped back from the table. "You're up."

I put some chalk on the tip of my pool cue. I always use a *lot* of chalk, even though it hasn't helped my game that much so far.

"You *know*. Guys don't like girls who don't eat." I looked for a shot I might possibly make, but even though the table was littered with options, I knew I'd manage not to sink anything. "It's a turnoff. That's why I ate the ice cream even though it had nuts in it."

I leaned over and missed the shot.

"Wait, you're telling me you ate something you don't like because you thought it would make him find you attractive?"

I nodded, even though I was feeling a little embarrassed. It's one thing to read an article called "Be Irresistible to Him." It's another to quote it.

"Why didn't you just tell him you don't like nuts?" Rogier surveyed the table while I went back to my stool and sat down.

"Guys don't like girls who are picky eaters," I explained.

"Where do you *get* this crap?" Rogier was leaning far over the table, one eye closed.

I thought for a second. "*Cosmo, Glamour, YM, Seventeen*. And," I added, "it's not crap."

He pulled his stick back smoothly at the elbow and snapped it at the cue ball. A striped ball rolled neatly into the corner pocket. "So you're saying you'll eat food you don't like just so a guy won't think you're a picky eater?" he asked, standing up. "What if you were allergic to nuts? Would you go into anaphylactic shock just so you could have a guy like you for two minutes right before you *died*?"

"Nobody's *dying*, Rogier. I'm just asking for a little advice, that's all. Would it kill you to be helpful for one second?" I couldn't believe how dense he was being.

Rogier leaned on his cue stick for a minute and pursed his lips. "Okay. If you want my opinion, eating ice cream with nuts is not going to be the thing that advances your relationship with this guy to the next level." He laughed at how clever he was, then took a shot and sank yet another ball.

"Gee, thanks, Rogier. That hadn't occurred to me." I remembered my fantasy about Josh confessing his undying love for me at my brother's funeral. Had I actually been feeling *guilty* for imagining him dead?

I decided to give it one more try. "Like, okay. How did you and Larissa get together?"

"She asked me out." Rogier didn't look the least bit embarrassed by this, but I was shocked.

"She did what?"

He was surveying the table again. "Look, Jan, if this guy is anything like me or any of the guys I know, he'd probably appreciate your making the first move."

I couldn't help laughing. Because if there is one thing Josh definitely is *not*, it's anything like Rogier.

Or his dorky friends.

It was hard to muster up any disappointment when Rogier finally sank the eight ball and defeated me for the fourth time that night. Neither one of us said much on the way home, but just before he unlocked our front door, Rogier turned to me.

"Look, I'm sorry I was so flip before." He put his hand on my shoulder. "Relationships can be complicated. I'm sure that soon you'll have a boyfriend and you'll feel comfortable just being yourself around him."

I looked at Rogier. Had I really dreamed of having a "wise" older brother who would dispense insight from the lofty heights provided by our two-year age gap? Had I, in fact, longed to go to this person for help navigating the world of love and romance?

If so, it was a shame because now that he was patting me on the shoulder and offering comfort and advice, all I really wanted to do was strangle him.

CHAPTER FIFTEEN

Once again I have Mr. Kryle to thank for the latest development in my (nonexistent) love life. In September, when I saw I'd gotten him for English, I actually hugged my guidance counselor. When I think of how perfect my life would be today if only I'd gotten Mr. "Don't I Resemble Tom Cruise" Perkins or Miss Muller the human fossil, I want to travel back in time and slap myself silly.

Monday started off uneventfully enough. I wasn't even sorry to be back in school despite the fact that my best friend wasn't speaking to me and my crush was mad because I didn't want to have his freak midget cousin for a boyfriend. Considering all I'd done over the Thanksgiving break was play pool with my brother and go to the movies with my parents, I didn't exactly see what I had to be thankful for.

In English, we started off talking about a character in *The Sound and the Fury* who meets his sister's fiancé and immediately hates him. Suddenly Mark Jacobs said, "That is *so* screwed up. How can he tell if he hates the guy after five minutes?"

Mr. Kryle laughed. "Are you telling me you don't judge people you've just met?"

"You can't go by first impressions," said Mark. "People's true value is hidden."

Mark Jacobs is the kind of guy who rates girls on a scale of one to ten based on things like how big their breasts are. There was no way any sane human being could let his comment stand. I felt compelled to speak.

"Mark," I said, "you are so full of crap." Everyone started laughing and turned to look at me, which I guess is what you get if you don't say anything for weeks and then suddenly come out with a real intellectual whopper. Mark laughed along with the rest of the class—he knew he was being totally full of it.

But right when everyone was still laughing, Josh said to me, "So, what? It's not important to know someone before you judge them?"

"Well, I mean, if you've never *met* them, you shouldn't judge them. But if you *meet* a person, you can judge if you like him or not." *For example, if he spends two hours staring at your chest you might decide you don't like him.* "Like, take . . ." I tried to think of an example that was *not* Henry.

"Think of Romeo and Juliet," suggested Mr. Kryle. I guess that was his idea of helpful.

"But that's different," I said. "That was love at first sight." I felt my face go red as I said it.

"Well, what was it based on?" asked Mr. Kryle.

"Yeah," said Josh in a really snotty voice. "I mean, would you say Juliet based her judgment just on Romeo's clothes, or did she take into account his overall looks?"

"Ah, *hello*," I said. I couldn't believe I stood accused of being shallow just because I didn't experience love at first sight with someone who spends his spare time reading *Barron's Guide to Selective Business Schools*.

Mr. Kryle just watched us, which is what he always does when the class starts arguing about something. Only this particular argument didn't seem to involve the whole class so much as it involved me and Josh.

"I'm not saying Juliet knew every single thing about Romeo from their first meeting," I said finally. "I'm just saying you can get a *sense* of whether you have chemistry with a person."

"*You?*" asked Josh.

"*Juliet*," I said, clenching my teeth. Why was he being so obnoxious?

"So you're saying *Juliet*"—he emphasized the word in a really nasty way—"proves it's possible to know right away whether or not someone's worth your time." Josh was leaning his chair back a little, and I found myself hoping he would tip over.

"Right," I said. "She could tell that—"

"Based on *what*?" Josh let the front legs of the chair come crashing down. I was almost afraid he might leap over his desk and hit me.

"Based on lots of stuff." I tried to think of specifics. "How he talked. How he acted."

"I know what Romeo based *his* judgment on," said Mark, holding his hands in the air like he was measuring out two fairly large breasts.

"Thank you very much for that edifying contribution, Mr. Jacobs," said Mr. Kryle.

"Did it ever occur to you that you can't get to know everyone *right* away? What if Romeo had been shy or—"

"I'm not saying you shouldn't get to know someone before—" I began.

"You can definitely tell if someone's cool or not when you first meet them," said Mark.

"Wait, what constitutes 'cool'?" Mr. Kryle asked.

"I don't know," said Mark. "You can't really describe it. . . ."

"But you know it when you see it? Like pornography?" said Mr. Kryle.

"I know pornography when I see it," said Mark. Everyone laughed.

"Is it what he wears?" asked Mr. Kryle, ignoring Mark's comment. "Do 'cool' people wear certain things?"

"Not exactly," I said.

"Yes," said Mandy. "The clothes make the man." Clearly Mandy had decided her life's ambition was to be a staff writer for *GQ*.

"So what if a new kid showed up and he was wearing jeans and a . . ." Mr. Kryle looked around the room at what the guys were wearing. "He's wearing jeans and a T-shirt and . . ." He looked at the boys' feet. "And cowboy boots."

Everyone laughed.

"*Cowboy boots?*" said Mark.

"Cowboy boots," said Mr. Kryle. He turned to Mandy. "And he asks you out. What do you say?"

"Mandy, you *cannot* go out with Mr. Wild West," said Jenny Rubin.

"Ah, I don't *think* so," said Mandy, taking a lipstick out of her bag.

Mr. Kryle looked over at me. "How about you, Jan?"

"The cowboy boots are going to be a problem," I said. "Does he wear them every day?"

"Every day," said Mr. Kryle.

"Because you can tell a lot about someone by his shoes," I said.

"That is *so* screwed up," said Josh. "I can't believe you think that!"

I couldn't believe Josh *could* believe something I'd obviously meant as a joke exposed some deep character flaw. I was so mad I wanted to scream, but now the whole class was waiting for me to answer Mr. Kryle's question.

"Come on, Jan," said Mr. Kryle. "This is your moment. You and your cowboy riding off into the sunset together. What do you say?"

"Don't do it, Jan," shouted Mark.

"Sorry," I said, avoiding Josh's glare. "I'm going to have to pass."

Mark started applauding, and so did a few other people.

Josh just scowled at me.

Rebecca was in Puerto Rico until Tuesday night, so even if she hadn't been not speaking to me, there was no way

I could reach her. The cruel irony of not having a best friend just when I needed her most was not lost on me as I sat in study hall (which I would have cut if there'd been anyone to cut it with), arguing with Josh in my head.

It's not that I run around making snap judgments about people like, *Oh, he's cool. Oh, she's a loser.* I mean, who knows better than Jan—the queen of the big-butted girls—that it's wrong to judge someone by how she looks? Who knows better than Jan—a girl whose closet is a sea of Levi's tags while her best friend's idea of a "little" shopping spree is a day spent at Barneys maxing out her MasterCard—that it is wrong to make assumptions about a person's character based on wardrobe? Me, superficial? Hardly. Prone to snap judgments? Ah, I don't *think* so.

I was at least twenty pages behind in *L'Etranger*, but I couldn't concentrate on reading. Richie was sitting a few rows away, bent over his book, making notes in the margins. I thought longingly of the good old days, when he would let me copy his French homework if things got particularly desperate. Desperate or not, you can't exactly copy a reading assignment. I pushed down on the binding of the book and forced myself to stare at the page.

"Tout de suite, on lui a demandé depuis quand elle me connaissait. Elle a indiqué l'époque où elle travaillait chez nous." Okay, maybe I had judged Henry a little on the white sneakers and greasy hair, but if he hadn't spent the whole night staring at my chest, talking about things being *provincial*, and mentioning his SAT scores every

five seconds, I might have been able to overcome his wardrobe and physique. I mean, I still wouldn't have gone out with him, but at least I wouldn't have spent the night fantasizing about stabbing him in the ear with a metal toothpick.

And let's not forget my willingness to reevaluate Tom Richmond's sex appeal once he decided to water my face.

The more I thought about it, the more convinced I became that Josh was wrong. It wasn't that I was *too* superficial, it was that I wasn't superficial *enough*. I mean, Henry wasn't the only guy I hadn't gotten a good first impression of. Hadn't I been pretty underwhelmed by *Josh* the first time we met? Hadn't I thought *he* was lame for a while, before I got all distracted by his stupid smile and his perfect green eyes? Maybe the lesson was not that I should *reject* my first impressions of people but that I should *embrace* them on a universal basis.

By the time the bell rang, I had vowed that I would do just that.

Which meant I no longer liked Josh even a little bit.

CHAPTER
SIXTEEN

Tuesday was without a doubt the longest day of my life.

In junior high we read this play called *Inherit the Wind*, which is about evolution versus creationism. At one point two characters are arguing about whether the day on which the Bible says God created heaven and earth was a twenty-four-hour day, and this one character goes on and on, saying, "Could it have been a fifty-hour day? How about a two-hundred-hour day? Could the day have lasted *ten thousand years*?"

I don't remember what they said in the play, but I can tell you my answer: yes, a day can last ten thousand years.

I went to every single one of my classes, but I didn't raise my hand once, and while I don't want to sound paranoid, not one of my teachers called on me. Even the woman who works the cash register at the deli where I bought a sandwich didn't say anything to me; she just took my money and gave me my change. By eighth period I was starting to get really creeped out about not having spoken a word all day, so in study hall I broke down and asked Mandy if I could borrow a magazine. She had *Cosmo*, *Glamour*, *Esquire*, *Entertainment Weekly*, and *Lucky*.

"I used to like *Cosmo*," she whispered. "But now I think it's totally boring. Have you read *Lucky*?"

"No," I whispered back. I half expected my voice to sound rusty from lack of use.

She handed me the magazine.

"It's *awesome*. It's just like a really long catalog. Do you like shopping?"

"I guess," I said. What I really like is going shopping with Rebecca because no matter where we go she always manages to find me something that makes my butt look okay and that doesn't cost a million dollars.

Mr. McMannis looked up from his *Daily News* to see who was talking. Mandy opened her notebook and started writing, and when Mr. McMannis went back to his paper, she slipped me a note.

I love shopping. *Lucky's great because when you see stuff you like, they tell you where to buy it. It's totally convenient.*

That is convenient, I wrote back.

We should totally *go* shopping *sometime,* Mandy wrote.

That would be great, I wrote back. I couldn't bring myself to underline *great*.

I tried to imagine a day spent going store to store in the East Village while Mandy checked off items she'd circled in *Lucky*. How long would it take before I got so bored my brain liquefied and ran out my ears?

When the bell rang I handed Mandy back her magazine. She tried to pin me down to a shopping spree over the weekend, but I told her my parents wanted me home right after school and I had to run.

It was weird to be at my locker without Rebecca again. Each year on the first day of school one of us finds out who has the locker next to hers and the other one trades lockers with that person. That way even if we don't have any classes or frees together, we always see each other at least a few times during the day and then right before we leave school. In September we'd gotten all teary-eyed about how this was the last year we'd have lockers at all, let alone next to each other.

How was it possible that three months later we weren't even speaking?

"Hello?" I called when I got home. "Hello! Anyone home?"

There was no answer. "HELLO!" Nothing. I went into the kitchen.

On the table was a note and a twenty-dollar bill.

Hi, Honey!
Dad and I are meeting the Colmans for dinner downtown—they're in town for the night en route to Paris!!! We should be home by 10 or 10:30. If you want to order in some Chinese or something, here's $20. Otherwise, there's sauce and pasta in the fridge. I got some ice cream, too. Hope school was fun. I'll try and call you before dinner.
Love, Mom

Here's twenty dollars? Here's twenty dollars? As I was

processing the implications of my mother's note, the phone rang.

"Hello?"

"Hi, sweetie. How was your day?"

"Fine," I said, knowing there was no way my mother would be satisfied with my terse answer.

"Great."

I couldn't believe it. What happened to expressing an interest in your child's life? Where were all those irritating questions? What had become of the never-ending need to know more more MORE about how her darling daughter spends her waking hours?

"Did you find the money I left you?"

"Mmmm," I said. "I see you're hanging out with real jet-setters."

"I know!" My mom laughed. She actually *laughed*! Like, *Ha ha, Jan. Even your parents have a more exciting social life than you.* "Can you imagine? One night in New York before heading off to Paris. Doesn't that sound thrilling?"

"I suppose," I said. "If you like that sort of thing."

"What sort of thing?"

"Oh, I don't know," I said, sounding bored. "That whole . . . Europe thing."

"Sorry to leave you to fend for yourself tonight," she said. "I hope you won't be lonely."

"Ah, I think I'm a little too busy to be lonely."

"Well, that's great. What are your plans for tonight?"

Rap thumped in the background.

"I have a *really* big test tomorrow that I need to study for." Had I actually been reduced to lying to my parents so they wouldn't know what a huge loser I was? How had my life come to this?

"They certainly work you hard, don't they, sweetie?"

"I guess." I started tearing little pieces off the note and building them into a pile. The music suddenly got really loud.

"Okay, honey," my mom shouted. Even though I knew she was just sitting in the sound studio editing with one or two other people, it sounded like she was at a really hip party for Def Jam Records. "I gotta go. Love you."

"Love you, too, Mom," I said, but I think she'd already hung up.

My little pile of paper looked exactly like one of the sand dunes on Cape Cod.

Why wasn't it still August, when my biggest dilemma was Coppertone versus Hawaiian Tropic?

Tuesday Night (The Plan)
1. Use twenty dollars to buy low-fat dinner (salad, tofu, etc.)
2. Spend evening working on college applications to ensure acceptance at superb undergraduate institution and future of fame, fortune, and happiness

Tuesday Night (The Reality)
1. Use twenty dollars to buy greasy Chinese food and pay for movie rental

2. Continue working through Jennifer Aniston's oeuvre with *The Object of My Affection*
3. Eat entire pint of Chubby Hubby

I wish I could say the low point of the evening was the moment I dipped my spoon into the Ben & Jerry's container and hit cardboard, but really that can't compete with the experience of my laughing parents walking in the door at ten forty-five, having clearly had a fantastic dinner with their fantastic friends from their fantastic college. When my mom came over to the couch—where I was deep in my post-ice-cream-and-Chinese-food coma—hugged me, and said, "Oh, sweetie, are you drowning your worries in ice cream?" I decided it was nothing short of miraculous that I hadn't moved out years ago.

I saw Rebecca before she saw me. She was wearing a black T-shirt, tight jeans, and platform boots. Her hair was up in a ponytail, but there were a few wisps floating around her face. She looked very tan and very beautiful and very, very It Girl. I, on the other hand, clad in cargo pants and sneakers, did not.

"Rebecca," I called. She looked up when she heard her name. When she saw it was me she stopped, but she didn't come over to where I was standing.

I started to get annoyed. Would it have killed her to take one step in my direction? I almost turned to go into school, but then I pictured us standing at our lockers, staring straight ahead, not speaking to each other day after day until the end of the year. It was too horrible to imagine.

"Can I talk to you?" I asked, walking over to her.

She nodded.

"Look, I'm sorry," I said. "I shouldn't have said that about you and Brian."

Rebecca didn't say anything.

"I know you guys are, you know, having a relationship, and I shouldn't have made fun of it."

She still didn't say anything. How could this girl possibly think *I* was the one who was being ridiculous?

"Maybe I *was* a little jealous." I looked away from her. She still didn't speak. "Anyway, I'm sorry." That was it. There was nothing left for me to say. If she thought I was going to fall to my knees and beg her to be my friend, she had another thing coming. My life without her was pathetic, true, but it wasn't *that* pathetic. I would not grovel.

I waited another minute, but Rebecca still didn't answer me. Her skin was perfectly tanned, and her hair had gotten blond streaks from the sun. But really, what can you expect from a perfect, skinny It Girl when you're a monster with a butt the size of a Humvee? I started to walk inside.

"Wait," Rebecca said. She put her hand on my arm. "I—"

And then Rebecca did something I had never seen her do before.

She started to cry.

* * *

"I just hate them!" Rebecca concluded.

We were sitting at our favorite table at Starbucks, the one all the way in back with the huge, comfy chairs. I like to think of it as "our" table, which is ironic considering I never think of the place I sit in French class as "my" desk.

"Was it like that the whole time?" I asked.

Rebecca shrugged. "Basically. I mean, they didn't really start fighting until dinner Friday night, but things were definitely tense before then."

"Wow." I'd spent so much of the week being jealous of all the fun in the sun she was having, I needed a minute to adjust to this latest development.

"God, they just fight about everything." She took down her ponytail and ran her fingers through her hair. "If my dad says it's a beautiful day, my mom says it's too hot. If my mom says someone we meet is nice, my dad says he's a jerk. It's like they're constantly on the lookout for reasons to be pissed at each other."

"Do they fight about you?"

"Well . . . kind of. I mean, like, my mom will say my dad is too wrapped up in his work to care about the family, and my dad will say my mom is too wrapped up in *her* work to care about the family, and I'm like, 'HELLO! This is your family speaking. You're *both* too wrapped up in your work to care about family.'"

"Did you *say* that?"

Rebecca didn't answer. "Do you want to know the *worst*?" She dropped her chin into her cup.

"What?"

"So after they've had, like, a dozen *screaming* fights

and basically everyone on the island of Puerto Rico knows exactly how much they hate each other, on the flight back my mom turns to me and goes, 'Wasn't that a nice trip?' Like I'm *retarded*. Like I haven't just spent a week with two people who *hate* each other."

"What did your dad say?"

"Oh, he *is* retarded. He was just sitting at his computer screen typing away like, 'I have no relationship to anything that happens around me.'" Rebecca put down her cup and mimed someone blissfully typing.

"Was it worse than usual? I mean, because you're always saying how—"

"I don't know." She took a swig of cappuccino. "It was just so depressing this time. I mean they made this whole big deal about how it's our last vacation before I leave for college and isn't it going to be special and blah blah blah, and then they behave the way they always do. I just totally hate them."

"Do you think they'll . . . separate?" I asked, avoiding the D word.

"God, I wish. It would be so much easier. But they'll just spend their lives torturing each other. And me."

"Maybe you should apply to college in California," I said.

"Yeah, or China." She laughed. "God, you are so lucky to have your parents."

"Are you *insane*? Believe me, I just spent an entire week socializing almost exclusively with my parents. You do *not* want them to be your parents."

"Why? Did they spent the whole time screaming about

how much they hate each other?" She took a bite of her muffin.

"No-o-o," I said slowly. "It's just that they're so . . ."

"So what?" She cocked her head to the side.

". . . lame," I finished lamely.

Rebecca smiled.

"Really, Rebecca. They're total losers. Believe me, after the week I just had, I know. If you still weren't talking to me, I was planning to join the Foreign Legion."

"Maybe we should both join," she suggested. "What are the uniforms like?"

"Unclear. And I fear a language requirement."

"What language?"

"French."

"*Ah, oui,*" she said, nodding. "That would be *un* huge problem."

"*Très,*" I agreed.

Rebecca stretched out her back and sighed.

"Look," she said after a pause. "I'm really sorry I was such a bitch about the whole Brian thing. I think I was just . . ." She looked at me and then looked down, toying with the edge of her cup. "I knew Puerto Rico was going to suck, and I was just feeling really tense about it. Anyway, I'm sorry I took it out on you."

"Don't worry about it," I said, watching her hand on the cup.

"No, really," she said. She waited until I looked up and met her eyes. "I'm sorry."

"I'm sorry, too," I said. We sat there looking at each other, and I knew everything was really okay between us.

I felt a huge wave of relief, like I'd been carrying something heavy and had finally put it down. Rebecca leaned back in her chair, smiling, and so did I.

"So," she said, "how was your week?"

"Well, as I said, I spent most of it enjoying quality time with my parents."

"Sounds fabulous," she said.

"Oh, it was." I told her about everything, including the English fight with Josh.

"So let me get this straight," she said when I was done. "He said you shouldn't judge people based on your first impressions of them, you said you should, and now you hate him?"

"I don't know if I'd put it *exactly* like that."

"Well, exactly how *would* you put it?" Rebecca scraped off the foam from inside her cup and licked her finger.

"I'd say he thinks I'm a bitch because I won't go out with his *humongous* loser of a cousin, and his judgment of me makes him an incredible jerk." I mumbled the last word because I had a huge chunk of Rebecca's muffin in my mouth.

"A what?"

I swallowed. "A jerk. Which is why I am officially over him."

Rebecca raised an eyebrow at me. It's an amazing trick she has, keeping one eyebrow down while the other one disappears up under her bangs. I've practiced doing it in front of the mirror, but I just look like I have to go to the bathroom.

"Don't give me the eyebrow," I said, finishing the muffin. "Really. It's over."

"Fine," she said. "You're over him."

"Right."

"Totally." She didn't look convinced.

"*Totally*. I'm *serious*. I don't see why I, a smart, funny, talented woman, should spend all my time thinking about some guy I—"

"What's your talent?"

"What?"

"You said 'talented.' What's your talent?"

"Well, maybe I haven't had time to *develop* my talent because I spend all my time analyzing the behavior of stupid, annoying, judgmental guys. I've decided to devote my life to my work."

"Don't forget more quality time with your parents."

"Okay, I admit that was a bad call." I finished my cappuccino and put down my cup with a bang (or as much of a bang as a paper cup can make). "But the work thing is for real. I'm going to get into an awesome school, work incredibly hard, and win the Nobel Peace Prize."

Rebecca kept looking at me.

"What?"

"So I guess cutting French is part of your new work ethic?"

I hadn't thought about that. "Well, it's like . . . you know how in Native American art there's always got to be one flaw because only God is perfect?"

"I thought Native Americans don't believe in God."

"I'm not sure."

"Oh." There was a pause.

"Well, maybe it's Buddhist art," I offered.

"I don't think Buddhists have art."

I was starting to get annoyed. "Well, Hindu, then. The point is that the artist builds in a flaw right at the beginning. It's part of the art. The rest of the piece is that much better because of the initial flaw."

"So what are you saying? That cutting French is part of your plan to win a Nobel Prize?"

"Exactly," I said. "It's the flaw that makes my plan perfect."

CHAPTER
SEVENTEEN

The truth is, it's very hard not to think about someone.

For example, it had become my habit upon arriving in English to look for Josh. If he wasn't there, I would think, *Where's Josh?* But now I couldn't think, *Where's Josh?* because that would mean I was thinking about Josh. So instead of thinking, *Where's Josh?* I had to think, *I'm not going to wonder where Josh is.*

But really that's kind of thinking about him, too. I mean, when you think about it.

On Wednesday night I actually managed to forget about Josh for two whole hours because Richie called to tell me Madame had taken advantage of my absence and assigned an essay on *L'Etranger*. Richie started reading me the essay questions over the phone, but I was in such a panic that finally he told me I should just buy *The Stranger* and he'd translate the questions for me on Thursday.

Thursday night my mom came into my room, where I was trying to decipher an essay Richie had xeroxed for me called "I'm a Stranger Here My/Self: (Post-)Colonial Algeria and the Phenomenon of Existentialism." He'd assured me the essay was the key that would unlock *L'Etranger*, but so far I couldn't find the key that would unlock the essay.

"Listen, sweetie, we might have a little problem with your Amherst interview."

"What do you mean by 'little'?"

My mom and I have very different ideas about what constitutes a problem, so *a little problem with your Amherst interview* could mean she wanted to drive up to Massachusetts on I-95 because of construction on 684, or it could mean the Amherst admissions office had burned down and they weren't taking applicants for next fall.

"Well," she said, sitting down on the edge of my bed, "I feel really terrible about this, and so does your dad."

"Yeah?" I kept my eyes on the essay. Sometimes it can take my mom a while to build up to her main point, and there's really no reason to pay attention to her introductory remarks.

"The thing is, your dad has a thesis defense scheduled for a week from tomorrow, so that means he won't be able to come up with us."

"Oh," I said. When my brother interviewed at Amherst, my parents made it this enormous deal, like they were the king and queen of a small central European nation returning home after fifty years in exile. I went up with them, and Rogier and I had to meet about ten million of their old professors and hear how they were both such *marvelous* students and such *marvelous* assets to the school and how we were undoubtedly such *marvelous* candidates since we had such a *marvelous* mother and such a *marvelous* father. Then everyone had to practically pass out about how much time had gone by since my parents graduated. It was pretty much the most annoying thing that ever happened to me or my brother.

Needless to say, I wasn't exactly heartbroken about not having the opportunity to relive the experience.

"I don't mind," I said, glancing up from the page.

My mom squeezed my hand. "Oh, sweetie, are you sure?"

I couldn't decide if I should express at least a little disappointment, since that would leave me well placed for a consolation prize if we happened to go shopping while we were up there. As I remembered, Amherst had some extremely cute stores, which might be worth at least a brief look. At the same time, too much disappointment might result in my dad's finding a way to reschedule his student's thesis defense, resulting in *Return of the Monarchy, Redux*. I decided not to risk it.

"Really, Mom, it's fine." I let her hug me tightly for a minute before shaking loose.

"Listen," she said at the door. "I was thinking of asking Pam if she wanted to go with us so I won't have to do all the driving." Pam is my mom's best friend.

"Sure," I said. "Whatever."

"Won't that be fun? Girls together!" She clapped.

"Mom, could you try not to be so lame?"

"Oh, you," she said, sticking her tongue out at me. Then she shut the door.

Sometimes I worry that, in fact, my mom *is* trying not to be lame, and what I see is the result of her best efforts.

Friday night I went over to Rebecca's. She lives in a

beautiful old apartment building on Fifth Avenue two blocks north of Washington Square Park. There's a huge lobby with fresh flowers and wood paneling and about a million doormen in uniforms, and then there's an elevator that takes you up to her apartment. I mean, when you get off the elevator, you're actually *in* the apartment: there's no other apartment on that floor *or* the floor above it, which is also hers. And in addition to there being dozens of rooms, each of which her mom redecorates about once a month, there's a gigantic terrace that wraps around the entire apartment (providing Rebecca with breathtaking views *and* an ideal setting in which to seduce her father's colleagues).

Rebecca was in the living room with her mom and a bunch of women, who were all dressed in identical beige pantsuits. She stood up as soon as I got off the elevator and came racing over to me.

"Oh my God, this is the most boring thing ever," she whispered. She was wearing a long-sleeved dress with little black and blue checks all over it. The dress would have made me look like a piece of upholstered furniture, but of course Rebecca looked gorgeous in it. "We *have* to get out of here," she said.

I waved at Rebecca's mom and followed Rebecca upstairs to her room.

"Those women were just giving me a whole lecture on proper skin care. They kept saying how important it is to *exfoliate* while you're still young. I was afraid they were about to strap me down and give me a facial." Rebecca lay facedown on her bed.

Rebecca's room is very modern: it has modular furniture and modern art on the walls and everything is white except for a few red and yellow "accents," as her mother calls them. I'm always afraid I'm going to spill something on the rug, but Rebecca says it would make her mother happy if I did since then she'd have an excuse to redecorate.

"I'm definitely going to fail French," I said, flopping down on the white love seat by the window. "There is not one thing about that language I understand."

"Perhaps because it's the language of love," she suggested. I threw an accent pillow at her.

"I'm telling you," I said. "I've been taking French for five years and all I know how to say is, *'L'oiseau est au seuil de la fenêtre.'*"

"Sounds racy." Rebecca sat up and rummaged around in her bag. She lit a cigarette and went over to open the glass door onto the terrace.

"It means 'The bird is on the windowsill,'" I said, checking my hair for split ends. A girl at summer camp showed me how if you find one you can snap it off and then the hair won't split all the way to the root. "Oh, and I can say, 'Hello, I'm Mr. Thibaut. Have you met my wife?'"

"Now, that's practical," said Rebecca.

"Tell me about it." I lay there thinking of all the other things I can say in French. *The boy has a red ball. I am an American. Today is Thursday.* There wasn't one witty observation in my repertoire. Even if Rebecca and I did take our European vacation together, how was I going to pick up sexy French guys if all I could say is, "Hello. Today is Thursday. Have you met my wife?"

"I'm thinking about having sex with Brian," Rebecca said suddenly.

"No way!" I dropped the hair I was holding and tilted my head so I could just see Rebecca out of the corner of my eye. It was hard to read the expression on her face since she was upside down.

"Do you think it's a bad idea?"

"Bad in what sense?" After the fiasco that was our last conversation about this particular subject, I thought it wise to tread carefully.

"Bad, like, bad. Irresponsible. Foolish. Unwise." She stubbed out her cigarette and closed the door. "Bad in the sense of not good."

"Look, I'm the last person in the world you want to ask for advice," I said, sitting up. "All I know about relationships is how not to have them."

Rebecca climbed back onto the bed and pulled a blanket over her feet. "The thing is, I'm going to have to come up with some pretty inventive excuses if I want to keep not doing it."

"Well, I think—"

She cut me off before I could finish. "I really don't even see what the big deal is. I mean, it's crazy to get all worked up about it."

"It does seem crazy," I said. I felt even less convinced than I sounded, and I didn't sound very convinced.

"I mean, it's not really like it's all that different from other stuff," she pointed out.

"Sure," I said.

"I mean, he's *really* cute," she pointed out.

"That he is."

"And we've done everything else," she said, answering my unasked question.

"Good point," I said. I'd been feeling bad for so long about being out of the loop that I couldn't understand how being *in* the loop was suddenly making me feel even worse.

"So it's not really a big deal." Rebecca seemed fine having this conversation with herself. She took a nail file out of her night table. For a minute the only sound was her filing her nails.

A few years ago my mom and my dad had this argument about about President Clinton's saying he didn't have sex with Monica Lewinsky. My dad felt like Clinton had out-and-out lied because he'd obviously had sex with her, but my mom said she thought it was more complicated than that. She said society draws a distinction between sexual intercourse and other kinds of sexual acts, like how adults tell teenagers they shouldn't have sex, but they don't mean they shouldn't make out or go to second base or stuff like that. She probably didn't say second base (I can't exactly remember how she put it), but that was her point.

My dad said Clinton wasn't a teenager, and for a grown man to deny that oral sex was sex was reprehensible. This whole conversation took place one night when these old college friends of theirs were over. Rogier and I were eating with them, but we weren't exactly participating in the discussion. I still remember when my dad said "oral sex," and Rogier and I looked up at the same time and made eye contact and then we looked right down at our plates. I must have been a freshman and Rogier was a junior, so it wasn't like we'd never heard of it before. Still, it was kind of weird to hear the words coming out of my dad's mouth. I think he realized what he'd said right at that moment, too, because the conversation pretty much stopped after that.

"I think it would be good to have sex for the first time with someone who's not a virgin," said Rebecca. I realized she had probably been waiting for me to say something, but I was afraid if I said the wrong thing she'd get mad at me again.

"Mmmm," is what I finally settled on.

"Don't you want to lose your virginity before college?" Rebecca got up and went over to her closet, which is roughly the size of Grand Central Station.

"Um, I think you probably need a guy to lose your virginity," I pointed out.

"Well, let's say a really cute guy wanted to have sex with you," she said. She took off her dress and pulled on a Brown sweatshirt.

"Oh, so this is one of those *complete* fantasies, like, 'If I had a million dollars.'"

Rebecca zipped up her jeans. "Let's say Josh."

"I'm sorry, I don't believe I know anyone by that name."

She gave me her exasperated face. "Hypothetically, let's say you and Josh fell in love and he wanted to have sex with you."

"Hypothetically?"

"Yeah."

I lay back down and started looking at my split ends again.

"So hypothetically this so-called Josh person breaks up with his girlfriend, asks me out, I say yes even though I hate him, we start going out, we fall in love without my ever speaking to him, and he wants to have sex with me."

Rebecca went into her bathroom and started applying eyeliner.

I couldn't actually see her, but I could see her reflection in the mirror. "You're being really mature about this, you know?" she said.

"I'll have you know," I pointed out, "I am breaking a *major* vow by even talking about him, much less contemplating having sex with him."

"Well, I really appreciate that," she said.

Normally I would have gotten up and followed Rebecca into the bathroom, but I needed to digest her announcement. Even though Rebecca had always been at least a base ahead of me, this was different.

I guess I agree with Bill Clinton: there's everything else, and then there's sex.

I got up and went into the bathroom.

"I guess you should go for it," I told her. "I mean, if you want to."

"I guess." She shrugged. I was ready to continue the conversation, but Rebecca was obviously ready to end it.

"Here," she said, handing over a lipstick. "Try this. I liked it at first, but it's too dark for me."

I started putting it on. It was a much redder color than I would normally wear.

"This is good," I said, looking at myself. "I look very sexy with this."

She looked at my reflection and smiled her thousand-watt smile.

"You look awesome," she said. "I knew you would."

I couldn't stop admiring myself.

"You look like a French Natalie Portman," she said.

"You *think*?" I pulled my hair back from my face and sucked in my cheeks. "*Ah, oui!* I *do* look kind of like Natalie Portman."

"I told you."

"You're letting me have this lipstick. You know that, don't you?"

"Oh, I know," she said. She looked at her reflection again. "Do you think I should grow my hair out?"

I looked at her critically. "Well, I liked it short, but it's kind of sexy now that it's a little longer."

"That's what I thought. Brian says he likes it this length, too."

Brian says he likes it this length, too?

"Are you turning into one of those girls?"

"What girls?"

"You know." I put on a high, girlish voice. "Oh, Brian says this. Oh, Brian says that. Oh, I couldn't possibly do anything until I ask Brian about it."

"I am so psyched for you to have a boyfriend you talk about constantly," she said, taking the lipstick from me.

"You have no idea how mercilessly I am going to mock you."

"Don't hold your breath," I said, carefully blotting my lips with a tissue. "Because it's never going to happen."

"I wouldn't be so sure about that." She went back into her bedroom and dropped the lipstick in my bag.

I couldn't help wishing Rebecca had never said, "Hypothetically, let's say you and Josh fell in love and he wanted to have sex with you." If only she had said, "Imagine you meet a really handsome Frenchman. . . ." Because the thing is, once you start imagining someone falling in love with you, it's kind of hard to stop. In English Monday, half of me ignored Josh, and the other half thought about what it would be like if he fell in love with me. On the train home Tuesday, half of me thought about how arrogant Josh is, and the other half thought about what it would be like to have him be my boyfriend. At Starbucks Wednesday, half of me listened to Rebecca describe everything she and Brian had and had not done in bed, and the other half thought about what it would be like to do all of those things with Josh. Wednesday night I finally came up with circumstances under which I could go out with Josh but not forgive him for the fight we'd had in English.

Scene: *New York City, a suite at the Plaza Hotel. Jan sits on a sofa by the fireplace, which has a fire going.*
Setting: *After a nuclear explosion.*

JOSH: *(Enters wearing a tuxedo and carrying a bottle of champagne.)* Jan! I can't believe we were spared when everyone else in the city died a fiery death.

JAN: *(Trying to storm past him.)* I don't care if we are the last survivors in all of New York City. I hate you, Josh Gardner, and I always will.

JOSH: *(Grabs her by the wrist.)* Don't be foolish, Jan. We need each other now more than ever. I'm not going to let you go. *(He kisses her. She resists at first, then gives in.)*

CURTAIN

It was daydreams like these that caused me to pay less attention than I should have to my mom's attempt to find someone to share the driving to Amherst. First Pam couldn't go because she was out of town on business for the week. Then my aunt Carol couldn't go because she had some big party Friday night. Then it looked like my dad *could* go after all because some professor on the committee was sick. Then the professor got better. The whole time my mom kept asking me to tell her who *I* wanted to drive with, but why would I bother to have preferences in the real world when my fantasy life demanded so much attention?

Which meant I, caught up in my increasingly detailed Josh-falls-in-love-with-Jan-who-continues-to-hate-him-but-not-totally scenarios, somehow managed to miss the key conversation that engendered the final turn of events.

CHAPTER
EIGHTEEN

If you didn't meet me but somehow saw my college interview outfit, there would be one and only one conclusion you could possibly draw: this girl gets dressed in the dark.

When my mom and I went shopping last spring for something for me to wear on interviews, I picked out a sexy but still fairly conservative short gray skirt and a tight black turtleneck sweater. I begged my mom to let me get it. It radiated cool sophistication. I could see interviewers from Maine to Georgia falling in love with my New York savvy, begging me to attend their selective yet terminally square institutions.

But after seeing me in the world's most perfect interview outfit, my mom decided to call the dean of admissions at Columbia, who's kind of but not really a friend of my dad's, and ask him what *he* thinks a candidate should wear. Like some guy who's about a thousand years old and probably doesn't even have cable understands anything about twenty-first-century fashion. And he told my mom that he would be "put off" by a candidate in a short skirt. "Put off." Those were his exact words. Rebecca said if you substituted "turned on" for "put off" you'd know how he'd *really* feel if I walked into his office in my little gray skirt. So then my mom made me get this skirt that practically goes to my ankles and has so many pleats it looks like I'm hiding a secret emergency butt in each of my pockets. And it's not even black or gray like the one I wanted to get. It's *dark green*. And to go with it, I have a *navy blue sweater set*. So now when admissions people meet me, instead of thinking, *She's so Carrie Bradshaw,* they're thinking, *She's so Laura Ingalls Wilder.*

The night before my Amherst interview (after my mom made me check to make sure my revolting outfit wasn't stained or ripped or magically transformed into something I might actually want to wear), I was watching *Friends* and talking on the phone to Rebecca. We don't talk on the phone during the actual show, we just call each other at the commercials. Unfortunately, we'd both seen the episode already, so mostly we were talking about the commercials and whether Sarah Michelle Gellar is pretty.

"I think she's too skinny," said Rebecca.

"You can't be too skinny," I said.

"You can and she is. She looks like a rodent."

"You just think that because you have a perfect body," I said.

"What does my body have to do with Sarah Michelle Gellar looking like a rat?"

"Well, it's like *you* can afford to be generous, whereas if you have a butt like mine you can't."

"You don't have a big butt, Yahn," said Rebecca.

"Okay, now try saying that like you're not reading it off a cue card."

The ad ended, and an ad for Chevy trucks came on.

Chiseled guys were hopping in and out of dusty trucks. I wondered if the ad was meant to appeal to women or men. "Would you ever date a guy who drove a pickup truck?" I asked. Now one of the chiseled men was climbing up the side of a mountain to get to his car.

"I think it would be kind of cool to *own* a pickup truck," said Rebecca. "I could have a cabin out in the middle of nowhere and a dog and a shotgun and I'd drive off-road in my pickup truck."

"I don't think you can find a MAC counter in the middle of nowhere."

"Are you saying I couldn't live without a MAC counter?"

"I just wouldn't say you're the—" Call waiting beeped.

"Hang on," I said. I clicked over. "Hello?"

"Elizabeth?"

"No, it's Jan."

"Oh, hi, sweetie. It's Sarah."

"Oh. Hi." It took more self-control than I knew I had not to spiral into a new baby-sitting-for-Hannah daydream.

"So tomorrow's the *big* day," she said.

"Um, yeah," I said. How did she know about my Amherst interview?

"I'm *really* looking forward to it."

I had no response to that. Suddenly I was getting a very bad feeling.

"Listen, will you tell your mom I *can* be ready at nine? I took care of the call today."

"Ah, sure," I said. My mouth was dry.

"Okay, hon. I'll see you tomorrow, *bright* and *early*."

"Right," I said. "Bright and early." Sarah hung up, but I didn't.

"MOM!" I clicked back over to Rebecca mid-shout. "I have to call you back," I said.

"What happened?"

"I have to call you back." I hung up the phone. *"MOM!"*

My mom *hates* when she's on the third floor and I yell something up at her. She's always going, "Don't yell. If you need to tell me something, come here." Usually what happens is I yell up at her, she yells back, and then I sit wherever I am for a while debating whether what I want to tell her is worth climbing two flights of steps.

Not this time, though. I yelled, "Mom! Mom! Mom!" and when she yelled down, "Don't yell! If you need to tell me something, come here!" I just kept yelling. She must have figured I broke my leg or something because finally she came running into the living room. She was a little out of breath.

"What *is* it?"

"Did you ask Sarah to come with us to Amherst?"

"That's what you had me run all the way down here for?"

"Did you?"

"Yahn Miller, sometimes you make me so furious!"

"Well, sometimes you make me furious, too!" I stood up so she wasn't glaring down at me on the couch.

"Why on earth would you be mad that Sarah's coming with us?"

"Because I—" What could I say? *Because I hate her*

son and I want *him to be my boyfriend?* "You told me Aunt Carol was coming."

"Aunt Carol was about ten mutations ago. I *tried* to tell you each time I asked someone, and you said, 'Stop bothering me,' so I did."

I actually had a vague memory of that conversation, but I tell my mom to stop bothering me so often I can't be expected to keep track of everything I've told her to stop bothering me about.

"So what, so now we're providing an Amherst shuttle service for other applicants? 'Hey, Josh, here's a nice school for you. Actually, they'll probably accept you instead of Jan because you can play a—'"

"Josh isn't going."

"He isn't?" I sat down on the couch.

"No." My mom went into the kitchen. I thought about what she'd said.

"Are you sure?" I asked finally.

"Yes, I'm sure." She came back in with a handful of potato chips.

"Well, fine," I said. I couldn't figure out why I was disappointed instead of relieved.

"He has a game he can't miss," she said.

"Fine," I said again. "Sarah just called. She can be ready at nine."

"Fine," she said, mimicking me. And she went upstairs with her chips.

Being sure—as in, "Oh, I'm sure Josh isn't driving up to Amherst with us"—is a funny thing.

For example, Columbus was "sure" he was sailing to India. Astronomers were once "sure" the sun moved around the earth. Many of the girls in my mom's movie were "sure" they wouldn't get pregnant.

So given that I am aware of all these circumstances under which people were "sure" of things they shouldn't really have been "sure" of, you'd think I wouldn't have been surprised when my mom and I pulled up to Sarah's house and honked and Sarah walked out the door.

With Josh.

Yet I was. I was extremely surprised. I was so surprised that in the thirty seconds it took them to lock the door and walk down the steps, I couldn't manage to find the words to tell my mother what I thought of her. It wasn't until they were actually in the car that I figured out what I wanted to say, and I was truly sad to discover my sense of propriety prevented me from blurting it out once Sarah and Josh were sitting with us.

"Hey," said Josh, sliding in next to me and buckling his seat belt.

"Hey," I said.

"Hi, Mrs. Miller," said Josh. Actually my mom's last name isn't Miller, it's Simmons, but she never corrects my friends when they call her Mrs. Miller.

Not that Josh is my friend.

"Hi, Josh. I thought you had a game," my mom said as she pulled away from the curb.

"Well, we lost yesterday, so we're done." His hair was still wet from his shower.

"I'm sorry I didn't call and ask if it was all right," Sarah said.

"Oh, don't be silly," said my mom. "It's such a treat!"

"Actually, we could *never* have come if Hannah hadn't *already* had a play date scheduled. What happened was . . . ."

I completely tuned out what they were saying, which wasn't too challenging considering how boring it was.

My heart was pounding. I snuck a look at Josh. He was wearing jeans and a sweater and sneakers. He looked comfortable and sexy, like he was about to go rock climbing or camping. I, on the other hand, looked like some freakish character in a children's book about primary colors. *And what color is the fat girl's sweater, Little Tommy? Blue! That's right. And what color is her skirt? Green! Very good, Tommy! Now, Tommy, can you think of a good word to describe the girl's butt? Big? Excellent, Tommy. That's a perfect word.*

Well, what did I care? I hated him anyway.

We sat silently for a few minutes.

"You look nice," he said finally.

I wanted to die. "Thanks," I said.

Sarah and my mom were talking about the routes they used to take from Manhattan, where they both used to live, to Massachusetts. Since we all lived in Brooklyn now, I wasn't sure why they were having that particular conversation, but they seemed to be enjoying themselves.

Which is more than I was doing.

"So, is Amherst, like, your number-one choice?" Josh asked me.

I shrugged. "I don't know. Maybe. My parents went there."

"Yeah, my mom told me. She said your brother goes to Yale."

"Mmm-hmm."

The drive to Amherst takes three hours. It seemed to me we'd already been sitting in the car for about six.

I am not going to make conversation. I am not going to make conversation. I hate him. I hate him. I hate him.

"So," I said. "Are you even applying to Amherst?" I know there are people in the world who can handle a lengthy silence, but clearly I am not one of them.

"I wasn't going to, but Ms. Kaplan put it on my list, so I thought I'd go see it." Ms. Kaplan is one of the guidance counselors.

"Oh." *Don't say it. Don't say it. Don't say it.*

"Henry said you and Leslie were applying early to Brown." There. I'd said it.

"Really?" Josh looked surprised. "Oh, yeah. I think I was probably talking about that last spring when he was out in Seattle." He laughed. "God, that's, like, ancient history."

Did he mean applying early to Brown or the girlfriend? I dug my nails into my palm so I wouldn't ask.

My mom turned on the radio, and the jazz station she and my dad always listen to came on.

"Hey, this is Sonny Rollins," said Josh. "This is a great song." Personally, I can't tell one piece of jazz from another.

"I'm impressed," said my mom, turning up the volume. "Do you know a lot about jazz?"

"Not really," said Josh. "My dad's really into jazz. I like Sonny Rollins a lot."

"Do you know *Saxophone Colossus*?"

"Oh, yeah. That's a *great* album."

My mom was so busy trying to look at Josh in the rearview mirror while she talked to him, I was pretty sure she was going to drive off the road. Ten minutes ago I might not have minded, but the latest development in the Brown–girlfriend situation made me want to live at least long enough to find out Josh's relationship status.

Not that I really cared, of course. I was just curious.

"Listen," said Josh after few minutes of music. We were on the highway, and the wind from Sarah's open window was blowing my hair around my face, no doubt turning my head into a natural disaster site. "I owe you an apology." He said it very quietly.

"You do?" I turned toward him, trying to hold my hair out of my eyes.

"Hey, Mom," he said, "could you close your window a little? Jan's getting blown away back here."

Sarah and my mom were deep in a conversation about the girls in my mom's movie. Sarah nodded and put her window up. My hair slowed down to thirty miles per hour.

Josh didn't start talking again right away, and it was all I could do not to say, *You were saying* . . . He sat tapping out the drum solo on his knee for a minute.

"I'm sorry I gave you such a hard time about . . . everything," he said, looking at me. "I was really a jerk."

We made eye contact for a second, and then I looked away. When I looked back at him, he was still facing me.

"Oh," I said finally. "It's okay." We were driving over the bridge, and the New York skyline spread out behind Josh.

"You were pretty pissed at me, weren't you?" Josh was smiling now, that smile I used to love back before I hated him.

"Well . . ." I said. I couldn't help smiling back at him. "Yeah, I guess I was kind of pissed."

He laughed his awesome laugh. "I could tell." Suddenly he made an angry face, squeezing his eyes together and frowning. "That's how you've been looking at me lately."

"How I've been looking at you? How about how *you've* been looking at *me*!" I scowled at him. "Hello, Jan," I said in a deep voice. "I think you are a total bitch."

We both laughed, and then Josh put his hand on my shoulder and squeezed gently.

If we'd had a sunroof, I would have floated out of the car.

"Seriously, though. I'm sorry. I shouldn't have jumped to conclusions like that. I was being a jerk." I was having trouble focusing on what he was saying. His hand was still on my shoulder.

It was like there was a switch inside me that I had no control over, and all the feelings I'd had for Josh two weeks before got turned on, while all the feelings I'd had two minutes ago got turned off. There was no warning.

One minute I hated him, the next I liked him more than ever.

I was afraid I might start laughing like a lunatic.

The car slowed down through the toll and then picked up speed again. Josh moved his hand away and looked back at the view of the skyline.

"Wow, look at that view," he said.

"You know, I've always . . ." I started to say, but Josh didn't hear me because my mom, who refuses to buy an E-ZPass, still had her window down from paying the toll. Sometimes I can't help but wonder what life is like for people whose parents actually live in the twenty-first century.

Josh turned back toward me as my mom put her window up. "Anyway," he said quietly. "It's a good thing Mandy told me the whole deal, or I might have kept thinking you were a bitch." He laughed and patted my shoulder when he said "bitch."

"Mandy?" I asked. What did Mandy Johnson know about Henry?

"Tom told her."

"Tom told her . . . ?" I had no idea where this sentence was going, but I had a feeling it wasn't any place good.

"About your parents." Josh lowered his voice even more. "You know. Not letting you go out with guys." Josh was whispering so quietly I could barely hear him. "You know, Tom and Mandy are kind of . . ." A few words got drowned out by a loud solo; I had never been much of a jazz fan, and Sonny Rollins's sax wasn't helping. ". . . curfews. We thought *we* had it bad, but then we agreed your situation is way harsher than ours." He patted me again, but this particular pat definitely communicated "I feel so sorry for you, Jan," as opposed to "I want you so bad, Jan."

I didn't want to laugh anymore.

I wanted to cry.

CHAPTER
NINETEEN

If Friday hadn't been one of the worst days of my entire life, it probably would have been one of the best.

When we got to Amherst, Josh and I were hungry, but my mom and Sarah wanted to go into a little antiques shop they saw, so they gave us money, and suddenly there I was, alone with Josh in a dimly lit restaurant. Even if Panda East isn't exactly the bar at The Madison, there's simply no way around the fact that it is datelike to sit across the table from someone of the opposite sex.

Unfortunately the pleasure I got from being with Josh on something that resembled a date was undermined by the fact that I knew I needed to tell him the truth about having lied to Tom. The things I should say to him kept running through my brain like my own private Muzak loop.

You know, Josh, about what you said in the car . . .

The thing is, Josh, I actually am *allowed to go out with guys, only . . .*

It's funny, Josh, because I think Tom might have misunderstood what I said. While I'm not allowed to go out with Tom, *I* am *allowed to go out with other people. . . .*

But each time I came close to uttering one of those sentences, I pictured him scowling across Mr. Kryle's classroom and I just couldn't say anything. Here was Josh shooting the paper wrapper from his straw at me, asking me about the tiny scar on the back of my hand, telling me about moving from Seattle, teasing me for being the only native New Yorker who can't use chopsticks.

I was supposed to give all this up voluntarily for a little thing like the truth?

The whole time we were sitting at lunch, I couldn't bring myself to tell him, so I vowed to do it as soon as we got outside. Once we were outside, I decided to tell him as soon as we were on campus. Then, just as we got onto the Amherst campus, I, being my normal klutzy self, tripped on a crack in the sidewalk and nearly fell. Josh grabbed my arm and said, "Are you okay?" He looked so concerned, I almost wished I had broken my leg just so he would keep looking at me like that while we rode to the hospital in an ambulance. (Of course with my luck I'd probably have one of those really bad breaks where the bone sticks out, and you take one look at what's happened and puke.)

"Yeah, I'm fine. I'm just a klutz," I said.

He held my arm for an extra second. "You sure?"

We looked at each other and the *Romeo and Juliet* scene, which I hadn't thought of in weeks, popped into my head. *Tell him. Tell him. Tell him.*

"Yeah, I'm sure." He let go of my arm, and we kept walking.

Amherst looks like a movie set of a college campus. There are stone buildings with actual ivy crawling up them, big old trees that tower over you, a white chapel with a bell tower, and, in front of the library, a quad that leads to the top of a hill with a view over the athletic fields. It was cold but not too cold, and we had a few minutes before we had to meet my mom and Sarah, so we walked to the end of the quad and looked at the view.

"Wow," Josh said finally. "This is really beautiful."

"I know," I said. "My dad calls it the Platonic ideal of a college campus."

Josh dribbled an imaginary soccer ball around the spot where I was standing. "I thought Platonic meant when two people don't fool around."

I didn't need a mirror to know I was turning bright red. "It also means the perfect example of something." The sky was pale blue, and there were a few puffy clouds high up. Even though the students walking by us were probably talking about how drunk they'd gotten the night before or whether the person they liked liked them back, it was easy to imagine they were having intense intellectual conversations about literature and politics. The air smelled clean and earthy.

Josh looked around. "I guess your dad's right," he said.

We turned and started walking back toward the library. *Tell him. Tell him. Tell him.*

"Wouldn't it be weird if we ended up at college together?" he asked.

I tried to look like the idea had never occurred to me. "It sure would be," I said. I could see my mom and Sarah sitting on the steps. *Tell him. Tell him. Tell him.*

But of course, I didn't.

* * *

Unfortunately, having 99.9999 percent of your brain else-where is not the best way to go into a college interview. Because, as one might predict, being distracted can cause a person to say things she might not otherwise say to a complete stranger.

And that can sometimes be a problem.

While I waited for my interview in the foyer of the admissions office, my mom, Josh, and Sarah went off to tour the campus. Just after three, a woman came into the waiting area.

"Jan?"

Rather than reviewing all the reasons I was a perfect candidate for admission to Amherst College, I'd been sitting there making a mental list of the pros and cons of telling Josh that I am a big, fat liar. Which might have had something to do with the fact that I looked up when my name was called and listened to the words "Oh my God" come out of my mouth before I could stop myself.

"What?" she asked, looking around. She was young and very pretty. I could imagine her in a *Town & Country* spread, one with a big southern mansion in the back-ground and lots of people lounging around on horseback.

I put my hand over my mouth. "I did *not* mean to say that," I said.

"Okay, I'll pretend I didn't hear it," she said, and she smiled at me. "I'm Lauren." I stood up and followed her into her office.

"Look, I can't resist," she said after we'd both sat down. One wall of her office was covered with *New Yorker* covers. There were tons of books everywhere, and

I saw several copies of *Barron's Guide to Selective Colleges* on one shelf. "What were you so shocked by?"

"You're wearing my interview outfit." She looked down at her tight black turtleneck sweater and knee-length gray skirt. Then she looked at me.

"I mean, that's the interview outfit I *wanted* to get," I explained. "It's what I would be wearing if my mother hadn't made me dress like Krusty the Clown."

She laughed. "Well, I'll take that as a compliment. But I don't think you look like Krusty the Clown."

"It's not that I'm obsessed with fashion or anything," I said. "I just had this idea of how I wanted to be in college, and I wanted it to start with my interview." Suddenly I realized what I had just said. "Not that I don't like who I am." Had anyone ever sounded like a bigger idiot? "Maybe I shouldn't have just said that, either."

She was nice enough to nod rather than laugh. "I'm intrigued. How do you want to be in college?"

"Cool and self-confident." God, I sounded like a *Chic* cover. *Chic and Self-Confident: We Show You How.* "I mean, I want more than that. You know, I want to be intellectually challenged and stuff." *And stuff.* She probably thought I was mentally challenged. And stuff. "But I wanted the whole package to look a certain way."

"I know what you mean," said Lauren, which was nice of her, considering even *I* wasn't exactly sure what I meant. "When I first got here I had all these skirts and dresses my mom made me pack. I'm from Kansas, and my mom thought that was how I needed to dress to fit in with all the fancy East Coasters I'd meet at school."

"Who were all wearing ripped jeans and T-shirts," I said.

"Exactly," said Lauren, laughing.

As Lauren and I talked about our moms and college and Lawrence, I actually forgot about Josh and started to feel happy. When she stood up to shake my hand, I couldn't believe we'd been talking for almost an hour.

"Well, it was very nice meeting you," she said.

"It was nice meeting you, too." Suddenly I had the urge to tell her everything that had just happened with Josh and get her advice. She seemed so smart and understanding, I had the feeling she'd know exactly what I should tell him to get him to understand why I'd lied.

"Listen," I said as we got to the door.

"Yes?" She had her hand on the knob, but she turned toward me.

The thing is, I really like this guy only I don't think he likes me. I mean, he likes me, but he doesn't like *me. Or maybe he does. But he might have a girlfriend. But the thing is he was mad at me because he thought I was being a bitch to his cousin only now he doesn't think I'm a bitch and so we're friends again only it's because he thinks something about me that isn't true and I was just wondering what you thought I should do about the whole situation.*

Lauren was looking at me with an expectant expression on her face. I knew she was waiting for me to ask a question about the student–faculty ratio or AP credit.

"I just . . ." I thought about the beautiful campus

202

and how much I wanted to get a thick acceptance letter from Amherst in April. "I just wanted to say thank you for . . . for not thinking I was completely insane with the whole outfit thing."

She opened the door and squeezed my shoulder. "Don't worry about it. I really enjoyed meeting you, Jan."

"I really enjoyed meeting you, too."

The car was parked right outside the admissions office. Sarah was sitting in the driver's seat, my mom was next to her, and Josh was sitting where I'd been sitting before.

"How'd it go?" my mom asked.

"Okay. She was nice," I said.

"What did you talk about?" My mom turned to face me.

"Mothers," I said.

"Uh-oh," said my mom, turning around. "I'm not sure I like the sound of that."

"Are we all *ready*?" asked Sarah.

"I think I've convinced Josh he has to go here," said my mom as Sarah pulled away from the curb.

"Yeah, your mom should get a commission," said Josh. He handed me a cookie. "We got you this at the campus center."

"Thanks," I said. I took a bite while Josh watched.

"If you don't want the whole thing, I'll finish it," said Josh.

"Okay." I took another bite. Josh was still looking at me.

"Um, do you want a piece?" I asked. I tried not to open my mouth too much since there was cookie in it.

"Only if you don't want all of it."

"Josh, you are *such* a pig," said Sarah. "You already had three *entire* cookies."

"But if she doesn't *want* it . . . Maybe she doesn't like sweets."

"*Everybody* likes sweets," said Sarah. We pulled onto Route 9. It was only four o'clock, but already it was dark out.

"Not Aunt Jenny," said Josh.

"Aunt Jenny's a *diabetic*," said Sarah.

"So? Maybe Jan's a diabetic." He turned to me. "Are you?"

"Diabetic?" I asked.

"Yeah."

"No."

"Oh."

"Do you want some of this cookie?" I asked again.

"Only if you don't want it," Josh repeated.

"I want you to say you want it," I said.

"I want you to say you *don't* want it," he said.

"Say it," I said.

"You say it," he said. What *was* it about that smile of his?

I ripped what was left of the cookie in half. "Here."

Josh reached for the cookie, and we both held it for a minute. "Now, you're *sure* you don't want this part?" he asked.

"I want you to have it," I said.

"You're sure, now?" It wasn't too dark for me to see how nice his eyes were.

"I'm sure," I said. He brushed my fingers with his as he took the cookie.

"You're the best," he said, popping the whole piece in his mouth at once. He reached over and patted me on the knee. "Really." He sat, silently chewing for a minute. "And let me assure you that next time we hang out, I'm buying you your very own chocolate chip cookie."

If there had ever been a snowball's chance in hell I would tell Josh the truth, it melted with that promise.

Josh finished eating his cookie and leaned against the door. In a few minutes I could tell he was asleep, and as we got on the highway I felt myself getting sleepy, too. The last thing I thought about before dozing off was this cheesy line from an incredibly dumb movie Rebecca and I rented once: *Everybody has a price.*

I couldn't believe mine had turned out to be a chocolate chip cookie.

I wasn't exactly under the illusion that one day was all it would take to turn me into the love of Josh's life, but the last thing I expected was for things between us to get weirder than ever.

I woke up just as Sarah was making the turn onto her block. Josh was already awake, but if he noticed I was up, he didn't say anything. As soon as Sarah stopped the car, almost before she had put it in park, he muttered something in my general direction that sounded like, "See ya," and practically leaped out the door. I was still half asleep, and my mom and Sarah had barely begun their epic good-bye when Josh, taking the stairs three at a time, opened the door to their house and disappeared.

Was there drool on my chin? I rubbed my hand over my face, but it felt dry. Had my sleeping given Josh the chance to observe my interview outfit in all its glory, thereby enabling him to realize I was part teenage girl, part circus act?

Was I doomed to spend the rest of my life trying to read the minds of schizophrenic boys who flirt with you one minute and run away as fast as they possibly can the next?

Mark appeared on the stoop with Hannah, who immediately came bounding toward the car. She opened the door and practically hurled herself at me, yelling, "Jan! Jan!" I'd never known a human being could bear such a strong resemblance to a Labrador retriever.

"Hey, Hannah," I said. I was still groggy, and part of me kept expecting Josh would come back outside any second. Maybe he'd just had to pee or something.

"I want Jan to be my baby-sitter again," Hannah yelled at her mother. "I hate Margaret."

"You do not hate Margaret," said Sarah. "It's very sweet how much you love Jan, but it doesn't mean you can't love Margaret, too."

"Don't you want to baby-sit me anymore?" asked Hannah. She looked up at me with her enormous eyes, and I didn't know what to say. What I wanted was to be too busy going on dates with her brother to be her baby-sitter, but the odds of that happening appeared about equal to the odds of my imaginary life earning me a Tony Award nomination.

"Well—" I started to say. I knew I had to craft my answer very carefully. You don't have to take a psychology elective to know kids can be scarred for life if they feel rejected in childhood.

"We're getting a puppy!" Hannah said before I could explain how I think she's a really great kid and my not baby-sitting her wasn't because she'd done something wrong.

"You are?" I asked. Hannah wasn't snuggled against me anymore; she was struggling to get out of the car.

"Oh, boy," said Sarah, leaning back against the seat and closing her eyes. "I was *not* prepared for this."

I couldn't have said it better myself.

I couldn't call Rebecca to process what had happened until I escaped from my dad's how'd-you-like-Amherst "chat," which consisted of him hurling rhetorical questions at me.

"Isn't it a beautiful campus?"

"Don't you just love New England?"

"What a fabulous town, right?"

I nodded until I thought my head might drop off and then made a dash for the phone.

"Hello?" She picked up on the first ring, sounding like she had run just as fast to answer the phone as I had to dial it.

"It's me. You won't believe—"

"I got into Brown."

"Oh my God!" *Say something positive. Say something positive. Do* not *start bawling. Do* not *start bawling.* "That is so . . . *awesome*!" I was still in the hallway, where I'd frantically dialed her number. Pieter rubbed against my ankle and I picked him up and carried him into my room.

"Can you believe it?"

Normally Pieter doesn't like to be picked up. He prefers coming to people on his own terms. But tonight it was like he sensed what a horrible time I was having and had decided to make an exception.

"That's . . . that's incredible." I lay back on my bed, and Pieter sat on my chest.

"Listen, I want to hear all about Amherst, but my dad's taking me out for dinner. He wants to talk about my going to *law school*!"

"But you just got into college."

"Tell me about it. Hey, do you want to meet me at Victoria's Secret in SoHo tomorrow? I need something for a"—she lowered her voice—"special occasion."

"Sure," I managed to say. "Sounds like fun."

"See you at two," she said. Then, laughing, she added, "It's all going according to plan."

I hung up the phone and closed my eyes, frightened about whose plan it was going according to.

"I've decided New Year's Eve is the night," she told me as we wandered through Victoria's Secret. "I know it's kind of cheesy, but still. . . ." She held up a lacy red thong, looked at it, then shook her head and put it back on the rack. "I think it's a good idea to start the year with a life-altering action."

"When do you come back from Belize?" Rebecca would be spending the week after Christmas bonding with her mother at a five-hundred-dollar-a-night spa. I would be spending that very same week bonding with unfinished college applications and my grandmother, who in all my seventeen years had never said much to me besides "Get your hair out of your eyes."

"We get back December thirty-first," said Rebecca. "My plane lands at five, and I'm meeting Brian at eight. D-day."

"More like V-day," I said.

She held up a black teddy with red feathers at the top and red pom-poms at the bottom. "Oh, yeah, something subtle," she said, laughing.

"Or maybe you'd rather go with a classic." I held up a leopard-print velvet bra and growled.

"It's so-o Lion King," she said.

I rejected a couple of tacky-looking black lace thongs. "Are you going to tell him it's your first time?"

"Are you *crazy*? A twenty-one-year-old virgin?" Rebecca checked the size on a pair of white silk underwear.

I handed her a dark blue bra with a little lace edging. "So I don't get it. What's the lingerie festival for if he's not even going to know something significant is taking place?" I had stopped trying to judge Rebecca's situation with Brian. Now I was just trying to understand it.

"It's *pour moi*," she said, grabbing a pair of underwear to match the blue bra.

"So it's like you're kind of losing your virginity with yourself," I said.

"That's a *lovely* image, darling," said Rebecca. She was carrying about ten different bra-and-underwear combinations.

"I think you can only take in six at a time," I said.

"So they'll arrest me." She looked at my empty hands. "Aren't you going to try on *anything*?"

I kind of wanted to try something on, but it's humiliating to buy sexy lingerie when no one is going to see it. Given the trajectory of my love life, I should have been at

Macy's, buying Lollipop underwear with little dancing bears.

Finally Rebecca convinced me to try something on just to keep her company, so I took one of the blue bras with the lace. We waited until we could find two dressing rooms next to each other and then went in.

The blue bra fit okay, and I actually thought about buying it. After all, how often can you find expensive lingerie that's as boring as your nonexistent sex life? But when Rebecca came into my dressing room, she vetoed it.

Actually, what she said was, "Yawn, Yahn."

"Yet that seems somehow appropriate," I said, taking it off. I still hadn't told her about the agony and the ecstasy of my day with Josh. I knew she'd be really supportive and take the whole thing seriously, but how embarrassing is the recap of a daylong he said/she said when the person you're talking to is shopping for virginity-losing lingerie?

"Try this one," she said, handing me a hanger and turning back to her dressing room. "It's too small for me." In addition to being thinner than I am, taller than I am, richer than I am, and more famous than I am, Rebecca, of course, has bigger boobs than I do.

Sometimes I think our friendship is nothing short of a miracle.

The bra she handed me was white silk with red piping. It looked cheesy until I put it on.

Then it looked *awesome.*

Normally I wear crop-top bras from Banana Republic. They're really comfortable because it feels like you're just wearing a tight T-shirt under your real shirt.

But this bra was a bra-bra. It had thick straps, and it kind of pushed my boobs up and together until there was a little V between them. I turned to the side. Somehow with my new boobs, my butt looked smaller.

"Let me see," said Rebecca, knocking. I opened the door.

"Va-va-voom," she said. "Jan, you look awesome."

I turned back to face the mirror. I really *did* look awesome. It was if I'd gone from Victoria's Secret customer to Victoria's Secret model.

"You *have* to get it," she said. "It's perfect."

She was right. It *was* perfect.

And tragically, nobody but we would ever get the chance to know that.

Christmas vacation, my sexy new bra notwithstanding, started out bad and got worse.

My grandmother arrived from Florida the same day Rebecca left for Belize. That meant right about the time Rebecca was settling into business class with her fruity cocktail and complimentary cheese plate, I was driving back from LaGuardia in a thunderstorm, while my grandmother described her newly diagnosed irritable bowel syndrome.

Some people worry about getting hit by lightning.

I longed for it.

Maybe I wouldn't have been so depressed about my train wreck of a vacation if the last few days of school Josh hadn't been totally weird, acting like Amherst had never happened. In English, I kept trying to make eye contact with him, but each time his eyes happened to drift my way he'd make sure they were focused on the clock over my head. I started to worry that my overactive imagination had invented our day together. By the very last day of school, when Josh zipped by me as we were leaving the Christmas assembly without so much as a "Have a great vacation," I was pretty sure I was bordering on complete insanity.

Actually, I wasn't the only one with a tenuous hold on her mental well-being. After twenty-four hours of my grandmother's complaining and criticizing, my mom started to lose it, pulling at her hair, rolling her eyes, and muttering things under her breath.

She was like a cross between a teenager and a homeless person.

"I don't see why Rogier had to go skiing with his friends. It's not like I come up from Florida every day." It was the second night of my grandmother's visit, and we were sitting at the kitchen table eating cheese and crackers and trying to decide if we should go out for dinner or order in.

"Ma, it's nice that he's made so many friends at school," said my mother, even though she'd been complaining to my dad about the exact same thing only two days ago.

"What?" said my grandmother. She doesn't hear very well, but she's too vain to wear a hearing aid. I don't really see what the point of being vain is when you're about a thousand years old, but my mom says maybe when we're that age we'll understand.

My mom shouted this time. "I SAID IT'S NICE THAT HE'S MADE SO MANY FRIENDS AT SCHOOL."

My grandmother shrugged.

"We'll just have to have a good time without Rogier," my mom said loudly. "*He's* the one who's missing out." Her voice was cheery, but I caught her digging her nails into her palm the way I do when I'm trying not to strangle someone (usually her).

"We made a reservation for tomorrow night at that restaurant you liked so much last time," shouted my dad, opening a bottle of wine. His voice was unnaturally cheery, too.

"What restaurant?" asked my grandmother.

"The French one," said my mom. "The one with the blue tablecloths you said were so pretty, remember?"

"I don't like French food," said my grandmother, brushing some crumbs off her shirt. She looked out the window at the rain that was coming down again. "It's raining so *hard*. It was sunny and eighty in Florida when I left."

I caught my mom and dad rolling their eyes at each other. "Don't you remember Les Trois Canards, Mom?" said my dad. "You said normally you hate French food and then after dinner you said it was your new favorite restaurant? You had the roast chicken?"

My grandmother shrugged again. "I don't usually like French food," was all she said.

"Jan really enjoyed visiting Amherst," said my mom, changing the subject. She looked at my dad a little too gratefully when he handed her a glass of wine. I think if anything could turn my parents into alcoholics it would be my grandmother's annual visit. "We went up there a couple of weeks ago, and she had a very good interview."

"You both went to school there," said my grandmother, as if my parents might have forgotten where they went to college. Then she turned to me. "You're going to Amherst?" she asked.

"If I get in, Grandma," I said.

"It's very hard to get in there," she said.

Leave it to my grandmother to forget everything in the world except the Amherst admissions statistics.

I thought I would have to beg my parents to let me out of dinner at Les Trois Canards, but when I went up to their room to talk to them later that night they were shockingly cool about it.

My mom had *The New Yorker* on her lap and my dad had a book next to him, but somehow I got the feeling they hadn't been reading so much as recovering. At first when I asked not to go to dinner my mom started to say no, but then my dad said, "Elizabeth, come on. It's her vacation, too." Then he patted the bed next to him. I went and sat down.

"You're holding up like a champ," he said. "Your brother owes you big time." He took off his glasses and rubbed the bridge of his nose.

"I guess it can be tough to be around Grandma sometimes," my mom said finally.

My dad took her hand. "Honey, you are a master of understatement." They both laughed.

"Okay, Jan," she said. "You can have the night off." My dad winked at me.

"Thanks," I said to her. "I owe you one."

As I was leaving, she said to my dad, "I hope I'm not like that when I get old."

I considered telling her she'd better be careful because she was already showing some irritating qualities, but then I thought that might not be the most diplomatic response. Plus my get-out-of-jail-free pass made me feel generous.

"Don't worry, Ma," I said. "You're *nothing* like Grandma."

"Phew," she said, wiping her forehead.

"Of course, you *could* try being a little more—"

"Watch it, kid," she said, aiming her magazine at me.

"I hear you," I said, mock bowing my way out the door. "I hear you, oh Great and Respected Mother of Mine."

"That's more like it."

After spending the entire next day failing to complete even one college essay, the last thing I was in the mood to do was listen to my parents explain to my grandmother that I wouldn't be joining them for dinner at her favorite restaurant (except she couldn't *remember* it was her favorite restaurant). I had seventy dollars of Hanukkah money burning a hole in my pocket, so I decided I'd do a little window shopping, rent a video, and then go by Szechuan Palace and pick up a cozy Chinese dinner for one. I was so grateful not to be spending the evening listening to my family scream banalities across a table at Les Trois Canards, I couldn't even be depressed about having nothing but Szechuan chicken and *She's the One* in my immediate future. I even decided to wear my new bra to celebrate my night of freedom.

There were no clothes worth trying on at Cutie Pie. At Sleeping Beauty, I tried on a sweater, but it had a strange zipper thing happening at the waist, so I just headed over to Video Express without any new purchases. There was a whole section of foreign new releases, and for a minute I considered renting a French movie. Perhaps just a few hours with Jean-Luc Godard were all it would take to turn me into a master of that elusive tongue. Then I thought about how hard I'd been working all day and decided to get *Sex and the City: The Complete Third Season Volume 1* instead. Maybe I didn't *have* an exciting, urbane social life, but at least I could enjoy one vicariously.

It was warm and cozy inside Szechuan Palace, and it smelled of garlic. I stood at the counter reading the take-out menu, trying to decide if I should stick with Szechuan chicken or expand my horizons. On the one hand, it's bad to get into a rut. On the other—

"Jan?" I turned around. Josh was sitting at a corner table. Sitting next to him was a beautiful girl I didn't recognize.

Across the table from them was someone I did.

CHAPTER
TWENTY-ONE

Josh was wearing his Brown sweatshirt and his hair was rumpled, as if he hadn't showered since he woke up. He didn't look especially glad to see me.

"Hey," I called. I didn't know if it was being inside in my heavy jacket or seeing Josh, but suddenly I was sweating.

A lot.

Henry waved, and I nodded in his general direction.

The beautiful girl beckoned me over.

I've heard that chickens, after you cut their heads off, continue to run around before they die. I guess it was the same physiology that enabled me to walk across the restaurant even though every one of my major organs had ceased to function.

"Hi," she said when I got to the table. "I'm Leslie."

"I'm Jan," I said, thinking, *Of course you are.* Josh toyed with his fork and looked past my shoulder, staring at nothing.

I wanted to be staring at nothing, too, but that would have meant I'd have to stop staring at Leslie, which was clearly impossible. I'd been wrong about her being blond, but every other fear I'd had turned out to be one hundred percent correct. She was dressed the way I'd been dressed the night I baby-sat Hannah, only where I had been pseudo-nature girl, Leslie was the real thing. The faded T-shirt she was wearing was clearly faded from use, not courtesy of Old Navy, and it was tight enough to show her boobs didn't need any help from Victoria's Secret. She had creamy skin, the kind that's just a tiny bit rosy even without blush, and brownish-red hair that was parted in the middle and hung down past her shoulders.

Needless to say, it was straight.

For a second I thought I might actually faint. At first I was *afraid* that I would, then I hoped I would. After all, what could have been a faster ticket out of this nightmare than losing consciousness? But of course I didn't.

You never faint when you want to.

"Why don't you join us?" asked Leslie. Her teeth were white and shiny. I wiped my forehead and my hand came away damp, just as I'd feared.

Josh still wasn't looking at me, which I couldn't really be too sad about considering my face was producing more oil than Saudi Arabia.

"Um, okay." I pulled out the chair next to Henry and sat down across from Leslie.

"Hey," said Henry.

"Hey," I said. He looked exactly the way I remembered him looking except instead of wearing a suit he was wearing a T-shirt of Josh's. I don't know if he'd worn it because he had run out of clothes or because he thought it looked cool, but whatever his motivation the effect was grotesque. He looked like a little boy playing dress-up in his dad's clothing.

A greasy, acne-ridden, squeaking little boy playing dress-up in his dad's clothing.

"Don't you want to take your coat off?" asked Leslie.

"Oh, yeah. Sure." I was a little worried about how obvious my new bra would be in just a T-shirt, but since neither Henry nor Josh was looking my way the concern seemed moot.

Leslie smiled across the table at me from her seat next to Josh.

"It's so nice to finally meet you," she said. "Josh talks about you all the time." Only a girl who looked like Leslie could utter that sentence without a trace of jealousy. It was like she was saying, *Josh talks about you all the time, but I don't care because I look the way I look and you look the way you look.*

"Yeah," I managed to choke out. "It's nice to finally meet *you.*" I wanted to add, *Josh rarely mentions you,* but I refrained.

I considered fake fainting. I could just collapse and then say something about how I had forgotten to take my medication and needed to get home immediately.

"Are you hungry?" asked Leslie.

"What?" I asked, even though I had heard her.

"Do you want some of this? I can never eat a whole one." She pointed at the egg roll on her plate.

"Oh, no thanks." Who can't eat a whole egg roll?

"You should eat with us. That would be so-o-o fun. You could tell me what Josh is like in New York." She jokingly punched Josh on the arm and giggled. Was it my imagination or were we getting into Mandy Johnson

territory? "Josh hardly tells me *anything* about his life."
She looked at Henry. "And Henry doesn't have *any* gossip for me. It's *so-o-o* boring."

Henry shrugged. Josh started rolling the paper from his straw into a little ball. I thought of our lunch at Panda East the day of my Amherst interview.

"Oh, I can't stay. I, ah, actually have to pick up dinner for my family. They're, um, waiting for me at home."

"That's such a *bummer*," Leslie said.

"Yeah," I said. Neither Josh nor Henry seemed too bummed.

"Well, why don't you order and then sit with us until it's ready?"

"Oh, I—" But I couldn't come up with a reason I needed to sit right by the door until the food was ready. "I don't think they'll let—"

Leslie stood up. "I'll be right back," she said.

"You don't have to—" But she was already walking away. Her legs were so long and thin she could have been in a jeans ad, and her butt was as perfect as I'd imagined. Before I could say anything to Josh or Henry, she was back at the table with a takeout menu.

"Here you go," she said. "The guy said you could totally sit with us." I looked up at the man behind the counter and he waved at me, smiling.

Why couldn't I live in a country where the customer *isn't* always right?

Given that my brain was on autopilot, I didn't exactly think now was the time to start experimenting with new culinary combinations. I'd circled Szechuan chicken and was about to stand up and bring the sheet to the smiling man when I remembered I was supposed to be ordering dinner for my entire family.

What were the odds four people would be satisfied with one entrée and a complimentary container of steamed rice?

I glanced up at Leslie. She was picking individual strands of cabbage out of her egg roll and eating them. At the rate she was going, she'd finish her meal around the time I graduated from college.

"So, what are you going to get?" she asked. Neither Henry nor Josh had said a word to me besides "Hey" since I'd walked in.

"Well, I don't think anyone's *that* hungry," I said. I looked at the prices. How had I never noticed how expensive Chinese food is?

"Don't you find that people always end up eating more than they say they will?"

"Mmmm," I said, adding up numbers in my head. Leslie grabbed the Video Express bag I'd put on the table and peeked inside.

"Oh, *Sex and the City*. I *love* that show. Is that, like, totally what New York single life is like? Maybe I *should* go to NYU."

"NYU?" I asked. Hadn't Henry said she'd applied early to Brown?

"Yeah, I had an interview this morning—that's why I'm in New York. I totally loved Greenwich Village." She laughed. "I mean *the* Village. That's what you're supposed to call it, right?"

"I guess." I couldn't help asking my next question. "So, is NYU where you're going?"

"Maybe," she said. She looked over at Josh, who was studying his empty teacup. "Or Brown."

When she said that, Josh looked up at me. Our eyes met for a second, and then he looked away.

I couldn't stand this anymore. Without even looking at what I was circling, I marked up the menu. "Excuse me," I said. I brought the sheet over to the smiling man.

"You join your friends," he said, still smiling at me. "It's okay." He gestured for me to go back to the table. "We bring it to you."

As I walked back to the table as slowly as possible, Leslie was whispering something in Josh's ear. I sat down just as Josh said, "What?" and turned to her.

"Um, could you excuse us a minute?" she asked me and Henry. Before we could answer she had pulled Josh to his feet. "We'll be right back," she added, and then she practically dragged Josh across the restaurant.

Henry and I sat next to each other not saying anything.

"Well, this is a funny coincidence," said Henry finally, "you showing up here." I was staring at the bowl of duck sauce, so there was no way to know if he was looking at me or not.

"Yeah," I said, though *funny* wasn't exactly the word that came to mind.

I revisited my fake-fainting scenario. But what if Henry knew CPR? The last thing I wanted was to come up with a plan to avoid talking to Henry that provided him with a legitimate excuse to massage my chest, put his lips on mine, and breathe into my mouth.

Without turning my head, I snuck a look over at him. Both of his hands were on his lap and his body was stiff.

"Jan?"

"Yeah?" I asked. My heart was beating very fast. Was he about to ask me out? I snuck another look at him. He didn't exactly have a beard, but there was a little growth of something on his chin.

"The thing is"—he didn't take his eyes off his plate—"I kind of have a girlfriend now."

"What?" I was so shocked I couldn't even try to hide it. *Henry the Horrible had a girlfriend?*

He finally looked at me. "Yeah. I just wanted you to know in case you were thinking . . . anything." Clearly all that studying for his SATs hadn't provided Henry with the vocabulary he needed for this conversation. "I mean, we just started going out. No one really knows. I mean, some people know. Josh and Leslie don't know. But I wanted you to know because I know I asked Josh to kind of ask you if . . . but then I kind of . . ." He shrugged at how inarticulate he was being. "Well, you know."

"*You* have a girlfriend?"

"I'm really sorry, Jan. I mean, I liked you a lot, but then Josh told me about your parents and—"

"You have a *girlfriend*." I wanted to stop saying it, but somehow I couldn't.

"I have a girlfriend." He took one of my hands in his and squeezed my fingers. I was too shocked by what I had just learned to care about the fact that I was letting Henry hold my hand. "But I hope we can be friends," he said finally, giving my fingers one more squeeze before taking his hand away.

I couldn't help myself. I started to laugh, and once I started I couldn't stop.

Henry the Horrible had a girlfriend.

Henry the Horrible was rejecting me.

I was officially the hugest loser on the entire planet.

"What's so funny?" It was Leslie. She and Josh stood next to the table holding hands, a sight that sobered me right up.

"Nothing," I said, staring at their fingers.

"Listen," said Leslie. "I just had this *great* idea. Why don't you come over after you eat dinner? We could all watch *Sex and the City* and then . . . hang out together." She gave Henry and me a knowing look. "You two must have a *lot* of catching up to do."

"Actually, we're pretty caught up," I said. Thinking about the "catching up" Leslie had in mind for me and Henry made me sick to my stomach.

"Hannah and Mark and Sarah are seeing *The Nutcracker*, so we'll have the house to ourselves," she continued, ignoring me. Her voice was cheery and fake, like she was in a really bad school play.

One that I, unfortunately, appeared to be starring in.

Just then the smiling man came over with two enormous shopping bags.

"Forty-four fifty," he said. My stomach sank. I took my coat off the back of the chair and reached into my pocket for my wallet, handing him three twenties. He put down the bags and took the bills.

I turned to Henry. "Well, good luck with applications and . . . everything." He smiled at me.

"You too," he said.

"It was nice meeting you," I said to Leslie.

The smiling man came back with my change. I picked up my shopping bags. They were a lot heavier than the cute new shirt I wouldn't be buying.

"Bye, Josh," I said.

"Are you *sure* you can't come over?" Leslie whined.

Josh finally managed to look at me.

"I'm sure," I said, meeting his look.

It was hard to pull the door open with a shopping bag in each hand, but I didn't want to deal with even the thirty-second delay putting the bags down would necessitate. I gave a gigantic yank and it opened, almost tossing me onto the floor. My jacket was open, and the air was cold through my T-shirt. I could feel my eyes starting to water from the wind.

I hadn't gotten more than a few feet from the restaurant when I heard my name being called.

"Hey!" It was Josh. "You forgot this." I didn't turn around while I transferred both bags to one hand.

"Thanks," I said. I reached out, blindly, and Josh put the Video Express bag in my hand.

"You know, if you want to come over—"

"I told you, I can't," I said. I took a step, and Josh grabbed my hand.

"Look," he said. "I—"

"You know what? Don't worry about it," I said. Now my eyes were really starting to water, and it wasn't from the cold. "Just don't worry about it." I pulled my hand away from his.

"Jan," he called, but I was walking away, and he didn't follow me.

CHAPTER
TWENTY-TWO

I spent the three days following the debacle at Szechuan Palace locked in my room writing college essays. At dinner each night my parents made a big deal about how hard I was working, and I didn't bother to tell them what was really going on—that I wasn't working so much as I was trying to burn a number of very unpleasant facts out of my brain, including

1. Everyone in the entire world was in a relationship besides me.
2. *Chic* magazine thought my best friend was one of the hottest girls in Manhattan.
3. I had been rejected by the grossest boy on the planet.
4. There were six cartons of Chinese food in the refrigerator with my name on them.

I was so grateful to the college admissions committees for coming up with their stupid, unanswerable essay questions, I wanted to write them each a thank-you note for allowing me to spend my time thinking about something other than how thoroughly pathetic my life was. *What is the extracurricular activity that has meant the most to you? What twentieth-century invention do you think has had the greatest impact on modern life? What is your favorite book and why? Describe a teacher who has influenced you.* Each boring, absurd question meant an additional few hours during which I could almost forget what had happened at Szechuan Palace.

Almost.

"Hey," said my mom, coming into my room. It was December 30, and I hadn't showered in three days. Soon you would need a pith helmet and a machete to cut through my hair. "Why don't you come to lunch with me and Grandma?"

The only thing I wanted to do less than be a pathetic seventeen-year-old single woman was to go out for lunch with the only other single woman I knew: my eighty-year-old, irritable-bowel-syndrome-suffering grandmother.

"I'm trying to get these applications done," I said. Normally I might have started a can't-you-knock fight with her, but I wasn't really up for it.

"I think it would be nice if you'd join us," said my mom. "She doesn't come up here every day." I couldn't tell if she was trying to guilt me or was just repeating what my grandmother said every five minutes.

"Well, I guess we can be grateful for that," I said.

"Come on," said my mom with a slight smile. "Come to lunch."

Lunch was as boring as I had expected. My grandmother told us a long story I didn't really bother to follow, and then my mom tried to tell my grandmother about her movie. But my grandmother kept going, "What? What?

WHAT?" so finally we just sat there in silence. That might have actually been a relief if my brain, suddenly bereft both of applications *and* mind-numbing conversation, wasn't free to replay, for the thousandth time, my last, humiliating minutes with Josh.

Needless to say, I was simply thrilled I'd been invited to lunch.

On the way home, walking down Seventh Avenue, we passed a vintage store I never go into. I usually like vintage clothing stores, but this one has ugly, old-lady dresses in the window, and when the weather's nice the woman who owns the shop sits outside smoking and scowling at you. I guess she isn't too up on modern theories of marketing, like the revolutionary idea that you're not supposed to frighten people away from your store.

Even without the woman standing guard it's a pretty unwelcoming place, but my grandmother's always trying to find this certain kind of cotton handkerchief she says nobody makes anymore, so we went inside to see if they had any. They didn't, and as far as I was concerned, we couldn't leave fast enough. The owner was sitting behind the counter petting an angry-looking cat, the kind that seems like it would be happy to jump off whatever it's sitting on and claw out your eyes.

And then, just as I turned to leave, I spotted the dress.

It was hanging on the wall and I might not have noticed it if the creepy owner-woman hadn't lit a cigarette right when I turned around. The flame of the lighter caught the beading on the dress and made it glow for a second. I walked over to the dress and touched it. It was black silk with black beads along the neckline and down at the hem. It had a scoop neck and cap sleeves. The woman saw me looking at it.

"That's from the 1920s," she said. Her voice was gravelly, like she'd eaten a plate of glass for lunch. "It's an authentic flapper dress." She took a drag on her cigarette. "They're hard to find."

My mom looked over at me. "Honey, we didn't come in here to get a dress."

The woman didn't say anything, she just sat stroking the cat. I had a flash forward to my life in a couple more decades.

"I bet it's expensive," my mom said.

We both looked at the woman, but she just shrugged. "Depends on your definition of expensive," was all she said.

"WHAT?" asked my grandmother, who was already at the door. "What's she doing?"

"She's TRYING ON A DRESS, MA," said my mother.

"She needs a dress?" My grandmother turned around. "What does she need a dress for?"

"For New Year's," I said, taking the dress off the wall. "For the party."

On New Year's Eve, my parents throw a huge black-tie party and invite everyone they know—people from college, the Cape, films my mom worked on a million years ago. Usually Rebecca comes, but this year she obviously had better things to do than hang out with a bunch of my parents' friends.

I, obviously, did not.

The dressing room was really just a little area in the corner of the store that had some curtains hanging around it. Normally I might have been worried someone would come in while I was changing, but with my mom, my grandmother, and the store owner all knowing I was in there, that seemed unlikely.

The dress was heavier than I'd expected, maybe because of the beads. The silk was soft, and as I slipped it over my head, it made a little rattling sound, like tiny castanets. There was no way to tell how it fit just by looking down, so I had to come out into the store, where there was a huge old mirror hanging on one wall. I walked over and stood in front of it, still looking down. Then I took a deep breath and looked at my reflection.

The dress was incredible. The neckline was low but not too low, and the low-cut back went down almost all the way to my butt, which looked shockingly small. For one second, looking at myself in the dress, I could think of what had happened with Josh and not want to die.

I knew there was no way my mom was going to let me get it.

"That dress is too old for her," said my grandmother to my mother. "It's not appropriate."

"She's just trying it on," said my mother. Even without looking at her I could tell she was clenching her teeth.

"You parents today," said my grandmother. "You let children grow up too fast. Then they take drugs."

"Mom, what are you talking about?" My mother was practically shouting in frustration.

"I know what I know," said my grandmother, crossing her arms.

My mom was fuming. Suddenly she turned to me. "Jan, do you like the dress?"

"Um, yeah." I tore myself away from my image in the mirror and looked over at her.

"Do you want to buy it?"

Was this some kind of trick?

"You mean, with my own money?" I had the feeling this dress would cost many viewings of *The Little Mermaid.*

"No, no, do you want *me* to buy it *for* you." My mom was talking to me, but she was looking at my grandmother.

"Um, yeah," I said again. Had my mother been replaced by an alien?

"Elizabeth, you are not getting that dress for her," said my grandmother.

"Mother, I am a grown woman, and I would appreciate your not telling me what to do."

This was without a doubt the weirdest conversation I had ever heard. It was like there was some bizarre glitch in the matrix that caused my words to come out of my mother's mouth.

"Well, it's your funeral," said my grandmother.

My mom and I looked at each other, and then we both started to laugh. We laughed so hard my stomach hurt, and when I finally stopped I saw my mom wiping tears out of her eyes. She came over to where I was standing and looked at me in the mirror.

"Sweetie, you look beautiful," she said. Then she put her arm around me. "Wow," she whispered. "Mothers. Are they a drag or what?"

"I don't know," I said, putting my arm around her. "Sometimes they're not so bad."

She took out her credit card, and I went into the dressing room to get changed. Back in my jeans I looked at the dress hanging on the hanger. It shimmered like it was moving, even though it wasn't.

And suddenly I was sad.

For the first time in my life, I understood what it meant to be all dressed up with no place to go.

CHAPTER
TWENTY-THREE

Just when it looked like there was nothing that could save me from the most depressing New Year's in the history of civilization, who should come to my rescue but, of all people, Brian.

Who dumped Rebecca at six-thirty on New Year's Eve.

"He saw the article."

"What?" I'd spent the day being ordered around the house from one chore to the next, moving chairs around, putting plates out, and searching through cluttered cabinets in search of something called votive candles. Now I was lying on my back, exhausted, trying to muster up the energy to take a shower.

"He was with his parents over Christmas and his mother had the *Chic* with the It Girl article and he saw it."

"What was he doing reading his mother's *Chic*?"

"He wasn't reading it. She saw it at the hairdresser's and she stole it so she would remember to ask Brian if I was his boss's daughter. She didn't even know we were dating." Rebecca's last name, which is also her dad's last name, is also the first last name of the law firm he's a partner in.

That would be the law firm Brian worked for last summer.

No wonder his mom recognized it.

"What'd he *say*?" Pieter was curled up on my chest sleeping, though I honestly couldn't figure out what excuse *he* had to be tired.

"Well, there was a message from him on my machine when I got home saying I should call him, so I called him and he said"—she made her voice really deep—"'Rebecca, I am extremely disappointed in you.'"

"What is he, your *father*?"

"I *know*!" Rebecca didn't sound upset so much as she sounded indignant. "Then he told me about seeing the article, and he said, 'We obviously won't be seeing each other anymore given that you betrayed me.'"

"Oh my *God*, he sounds like he's from the nineteenth century or something." Pieter lifted his head and gave me an annoyed look before settling down again.

"And it was *so* obviously about my being in high school. I mean, do you think he'd care if I *betrayed* him if I was twenty-five instead of twenty-one?"

I couldn't figure out why someone would bother to say she was twenty-five if she was twenty-one, but this didn't seem like the time to bring that up.

"Are you bummed?" I asked, scratching Pieter's head to make up for having shouted right in his ear.

"Not really. I mean, I was thinking about it, and I think my interest in him was just the result of my repressed rage at my father for being too involved with his work to notice me. It was very Oedipal."

"You're probably right," I said, smiling.

"So, can I still come to your parents' party?"

I couldn't believe it. "Are you *kidding*?" I sat up fast, knocking Pieter off my chest. When I tried to pull him back on my lap, he shot me a dirty look and went to lie down on the end of the bed.

"Well, yeah. I mean, if you still want me to come."

"I so-o-o want you to come."

"I'll get dressed and be there around nine," she said.

"Awesome," I said, hanging up.

Suddenly, it felt like New Year's Eve.

When Rebecca knocked on my bedroom door two hours later, she found me in the midst of a paralyzing hair crisis.

"You have to help me chop off my head," I told her as she came in the room.

"Okay." She was wearing a long silvery dress with a high slit up one side. "Do you have a chain saw?"

"I'm serious," I said. I was sitting in my desk chair facing the mirror on the back of my closet door. My hair was still wet from the shower, and I looked like a huge, unruly dog that had just gone for a swim in the ocean.

"I'm one second away from cutting this all off." I waved scissors threateningly in her direction. "You have to do something."

"Okay, okay. First off, do not panic," she said. "The doctor is in." She took the scissors from me and stood behind the chair, looking at my reflection in the mirror.

"Will you blow it straight for me?" I begged. Rebecca's the only person who can get my hair stick straight. She learned the trick from a Hollywood makeup artist she met at a party.

"I don't know." She was fussing with my hair, moving sections from one side of my head to the other. "Let me see what you're wearing, and I'll decide."

I opened the closet door and took out the garment bag with the dress in it. "My mom bought me this dress yesterday, but clearly I won't be wearing it since it leaves me exposed from the neck up." I unzipped the bag and showed Rebecca the dress.

"Oh, Jan. It's beautiful." She looked from the dress to my head and back again.

"I know, I know," I said. "You're thinking it's a shame someone as repulsive as me is going to disfigure such a gorgeous piece of history."

"Hardly," said Rebecca. She hung the dress back in the closet and took me by the shoulders. "I'm thinking, 'Have I got a look for you.'"

Forty minutes later, when Rebecca finally let me look at myself in the mirror, I almost passed out.

"Not to be conceited or anything," I said. "But I am totally gorgeous."

"You certainly are," said Rebecca. She'd put on a T-shirt and a pair of my overalls while she was getting me ready; now she took them off and slipped back into her dress.

But even looking at myself standing next to Rebecca couldn't make me feel any less beautiful.

Instead of blowing my hair straight, she'd curled it with a curling iron so there were long ringlets framing my face. Then she put the back up in a bun and pulled some wisps out, which she also curled. She'd done my makeup, too, giving me a twenties look she said was inspired by the dress. My skin was pale and my lips were a deep red. I was wearing a pair of very high heels and silky stockings.

"You should be in *Chic*," she said, looking at me.

"No, *you* should be in *Chic*," I said. "Well, I guess you *were* in *Chic*."

"You know, I think we're really just too gorgeous for *Chic*," she said, spritzing me with some perfume from her bag. "We should probably start our own magazine."

"Oh, definitely," I said, spinning around so the dress made its castanet sound, "with a sound track!"

By eleven o'clock I guess you could say the party was in full swing, except I don't think grown-up parties ever really get in full swing. You can always identify the climax of a high-school party because it takes place right before the cops come and everybody has to leave. But it seemed unlikely that was going to happen tonight.

Even with Rebecca there the night was turning out to be incredibly boring. There's only so much a hot dress, a great hairstyle, and a best friend can do to combat eighty fifty-year-olds and one grandmother. There was music playing, but it was stuff like Ella Fitzgerald and Frank Sinatra, the kind of music you really have to know how to dance to. For a while Rebecca and I faked it, taking turns leading even though we didn't know any of the steps, but that got kind of boring, too. Finally we just sat on the stairs and watched people. My parents were dancing together, and every once in a while they would start laughing and then they'd kiss. It was simultaneously sweet and revolting.

"There's nothing handsomer than a man in a tuxedo," said Rebecca, looking over toward the buffet.

"Are you serious?" I looked where she was looking, but all I saw was a sea of guys who looked like my dad. If you ask me, an old man is an old man with or without a tuxedo. "Those guys are all about a million years old."

"*He's* not." Rebecca pointed to the corner where our neighbor from Cape Cod was talking to one of the producers on my mom's movie.

"James?" James was only two years younger than us, but he looked like an eighth grader.

Rebecca nodded.

"Rebecca, he's a *sophomore*." I waited to see if she understood what I was saying, but she kept looking over at him. "In *high school*."

"Younger guys have a lot to offer," she said, giving me the eyebrow.

I couldn't believe what I was hearing. "I thought you said high-school guys were totally immature and a complete waste of time."

Rebecca stood up and smoothed her dress, which wasn't actually wrinkled. "Did I say that?"

"Rebecca, are you *kidding me*? You practically haven't said anything *but* that since September."

"Hmm." She thought for a second and then flashed me her trademark smile. "You know it *is* a woman's prerogative to change her mind."

"You're insane," I said as she started walking down the steps.

"Coming?" she asked when she got to the bottom.

"I think I'll stay here," I said. "But call me if you need any help changing his diapers."

"Oh, I will," said Rebecca. She gave me a little wave over her shoulder and crossed the dance floor to talk to James.

I would have gotten up from where I was sitting and engaged myself in conversation, too, but there wasn't anyone there I wanted to talk to. Plus, everyone seemed pretty happy talking to people who weren't me. Even my grandmother was deep in conversation with some old guy who taught with my dad at Columbia.

It was like watching all the animals climb on board the ark while water swirled around my ankles.

I was almost tempted to go up to my computer and work on my applications.

When the bell rang, I was feeling too sorry for myself to walk down the last few steps and get it. A woman who had been standing by the door went over to open it. I decided, rather than get trapped into making small talk with whichever incredibly boring friend of my parents had decided to be a little *too* fashionably late by showing up just before midnight, I'd better find a mirror and check my makeup.

I was halfway up the stairs when I heard my name being called. I considered making a run for it since whoever it was was probably too old to chase me, but then the person said, *"Jan,"* again, louder, and I turned around.

It was Sarah and Mark.

And Josh.

"Hi, honey," Sarah said, slipping off her coat. She was wearing a pale blue floor-length dress, and her hair looked blonder than it had the last time I'd seen her.

I was so surprised to see the three of them I couldn't think of a response; I just waved stupidly. I heard my mom call Sarah's name, and Sarah mouthed, "Happy New Year," at me over her shoulder before taking Mark's hand and heading into the living room. For a second I thought Josh was going to follow them, but he stayed by the door. It was like he'd come inside by mistake and was about to leave again.

"Hey," I said.

"Hey," he said. He wasn't leaving, but he wasn't exactly staying, either.

"I didn't know my parents invited your mom," I said finally.

He shrugged. "Yeah," he said. There was a long pause.

"Your mom looks nice."

He shrugged again. "We were at my cousin's wedding."

"Oh. There was another pause. "How was it?" My question sounded even lamer than it was because I had to raise my voice to be heard over the music.

"I don't know. Okay." He crossed to the foot of the stairs and put one hand on the banister and one foot on the bottom step. "You look . . . different," he said.

Different wasn't exactly the adjective I'd been going for. "Good different or bad different?"

"Good different," he said. Now he had both feet on the bottom step. As he stood there, looking up at me, I couldn't read his expression.

"Do you want to take your coat off or something?" I asked. He unbuttoned his coat but didn't take it off.

"Can I ask you a question?" he said finally. "It's something I've wanted to ask you for a while."

"Um, sure," I said. I had to swallow before I said it since my mouth was so dry.

"Why did you lie to Tom about not being allowed to go out on dates?" He wasn't scowling at me, but he wasn't exactly smiling, either.

"You came all the way over here to ask me that?" I said. "Whatever happened to 'Happy New Year'?" I thought he would laugh, but he didn't. In fact, he didn't do anything. I changed tacks. "How did you know I lied?"

He put one foot on the second step, and then he took his coat off and hung it on the banister.

"If I tell you how I know, will you tell me why you lied?"

He was wearing a tuxedo. The shirt was crisp white and the tie was beginning to come undone, making him look like a movie star at an after-hours Oscar party. Now my mouth was way too dry to say anything. I just nodded.

"Remember on the drive home from Amherst when you were asleep?" I nodded again. "Well, my mom asked your mom if talking to all those girls who got pregnant had made her be really strict with you, and your mom said she and your dad thought it was important for you to have your freedom and they just hoped you would make smart decisions." He had been looking past my shoulder when he said that, but now he looked at me. "That doesn't exactly sound like someone who won't let her daughter go out on dates."

"No, it doesn't," I said, trying to smile at him.

"No, it doesn't," he repeated, not smiling.

We stood there for a minute. "So?" he said.

"So . . . what?" I asked.

"So why did you lie to Tom?"

"I didn't want to go out with Tom," I said, meeting his look.

He took another step up. "That's what I figured," he said. "But then why did you lie to me?"

"I didn't lie to you," I said. "I just let you believe something that wasn't exactly true." My heart was beating so hard I expected Josh's next question to be, *What's that drumming sound?*

"And you did that because . . ." He was only a few steps away from me now. I had to admit Rebecca was right. Guys *do* look adorable in tuxedos.

"Why do you care, Josh? If you're still trying to fix me up with Henry, you should probably know that he has a girlfriend." I expected Josh to get all flustered, but he just kept staring at me.

"I know that *now*," he said, sarcastically. "And I never wanted to fix you up with Henry."

"Wow, Josh," I said, equally sarcastically. "That's *so* strange. Because just a few days ago, *someone* practically begged me to come over to your house and hook up with Henry. Isn't that *weird*? I mean, isn't that just the weirdest thing?"

"I thought you liked Henry, but you were embarrassed to tell me." He was practically shouting.

"Where would you *possibly* get that idea?" I was almost shouting now, too.

"It doesn't matter," said Josh. His cheeks were suddenly flushed.

"No," I said, crossing my arms. "I think it does matter, actually."

We stared at each other.

"Leslie," he muttered finally.

"Leslie?"

For the first time that night Josh seemed genuinely uncomfortable. "She said you probably *didn't* like Tom and that's why you lied to him, but you probably *did* like Henry, only you were embarrassed to admit it to me," he mumbled. "She said girls do stuff like that, and I owed it to you to help you two get together."

"She said that?"

"Yeah."

"And you believed her?"

He didn't say anything.

"Well, fine," I said. "You did what your girlfriend said you *owed* me. I really appreciate it. You're a prince. Happy New Year. Good night." I turned to go upstairs.

"She's not my girlfriend."

I didn't turn around. "What?"

"She's not my girlfriend. She wasn't ever really, you

know, my girlfriend. But now she's not even, you know, kind of my girlfriend."

I turned around. I expected to find Josh staring at his feet, but he was looking right at me.

"Why have you been acting so weird around me lately?" I asked.

"Did you lie to me so I wouldn't ask you out?"

My stomach dropped.

"Excuse me?"

Josh started counting off on his fingers. "When I told you Henry liked you, you said your love life was none of my business. Then you said all that stuff in English about knowing right away whether or not you have chemistry with someone. And then you let me think you weren't allowed to go out with guys. Was that all so I wouldn't ask you to go out with me?"

He was one step below me, and our eyes were level.

"I said my love life was none of your business because I thought you wanted *Henry* to be in my love life. I said you can tell right away if you have chemistry with someone because I knew right away I didn't have any chemistry with *Henry*. I let you think I wasn't allowed to go out with guys because I thought you wanted me to go out with *Henry*."

Josh leaned in close to me. "*I* wanted to be in your love life. I wanted to know if you thought *we* had chemistry. I wanted *us* to go out."

"Oh," I said.

Downstairs, someone had turned the music off, and all the guests were counting down the last seconds of the year. "Ten . . . nine . . . eight . . . seven . . . six . . . five . . . four . . . three . . . two . . . one . . . Happy New Year!"

We stood there as someone flicked the lights on and off, and I waited for Josh to kiss me. I was completely prepared. I knew he would put his arms around me and lean in and then slowly, slowly, tantalizingly slowly, our lips would finally meet. It was *Romeo and Juliet* all over again, only this time with a happy ending. Romeo doesn't drink the poison. He leans down to kiss Juliet just as she opens her eyes. They embrace! Tragedy is averted! Everyone lives happily after.

But Josh didn't move. I couldn't believe it. After all that, the night was going to end with the two of us one step apart just staring at each other.

And then, before I could think about it for too long, I leaned forward and kissed him. It wasn't the least bit slow. Or tantalizing. In fact, it was kind of abrupt. One second we were standing there, the next my lips were planted on his.

At first I thought Josh might be more shocked than glad, but then he was kissing me back and I wasn't thinking anything at all except maybe that those Fire Island books had been telling the truth after all. His lips were soft, and he tasted like Trident blue, which just happens to be my favorite kind of gum.

Maybe it wasn't exactly Shakespeare.

But it was good enough for me.

CURTAIN

Acknowledgments

For generosity above and beyond the call, whether of duty, family, or friendship, I am indebted to Neal Gantcher, Angela Nosari, Helen Perelman, Elizabeth Rudnick, and the Saint Ann's community—especially Stanley Bosworth and Ruth Chapman.